Big Familia

A Novel

Big Familia

Tomas Moniz

ACRE

CINCINNATI 2019

Acre Books is made possible by the support of the University of Cincinnati Department of English and the Robert and Adele Schiff Foundation.

Library of Congress Cataloging-in-Publication Data TK.

ISBN-10 (pbk) 1-946724-22-X   ISBN-13 (pbk) 978-1-946724-22-9
ISBN-10 (ebook) 1-946724-23-8   ISBN-13 (ebook) 978-1-946724-23-6

Designed by Barbara Neely Bourgoyne
Cover art: *Humans Kind,* © 2019 Rob Moss Wilson

The press is based at the University of Cincinnati, Department of English and Comparative Literature, McMicken Hall, Room 248, PO Box 210069, Cincinnati, OH, 45221–0069.

Acre Books books may be purchased at a discount for educational use. For information please email business@acre-books.com.

The spoken word was the seed of love in the darkness.

—TOMÁS RIVERA

You could press your ear to my chest
Find out exactly what you're up against

—"It's a Secret," Dark Dark Dark

CONTENTS

Big Familia

1

Disproportionate

As a single man in my late thirties, I'm aware that my belly should not protrude farther than my penis. At this point it's a tie.

So I'm on this health kick, trying to exercise more. I recently even bought a 24-Hour Fitness membership and started going once a month. I know I need to go more often than that. I just can't seem to break the once-a-month habit. That's why I'm on this bike wearing sexy spandex, hurrying home to eat the salad waiting in my fridge and drink sparkly water and be ignored by my teenage daughter.

But as I ride up King Street in south Berkeley, I see a fire truck and a white animal-services vehicle with lights flashing in front of Mr. Delbert's house. He's my seventy-something-year-old neighbor, one of the few remaining black residents in a neighborhood that was predominantly black. He's lived in his house up the street from my apartment—with a Rottweiler named Mr. Dog—for over forty years.

There's a small crowd of neighbors.

Hey, I ask a lady in a uniform, where's Mr. Delbert?

The person living at this house? They took him to the hospital, she says.

Is he alive?

Not sure.

One of the older neighbors shakes her head and says, It didn't look good.

I feel my sweat starting to dry on my body in the cool evening air. I watch the lights flash red and yellow on the houses and buildings. I hear a whimpering from the white truck.

I say, What are you going to do with Mr. Dog?

Take him to the shelter because he's a risk. He wouldn't let the emergency workers get to the patient.

I met Mr. Delbert at Nicks, the bar up the street from my apartment. He'd been going there for twenty-plus years. Nicks is the most painful shade of blue. The whole building: the walls and the trim and the awning, even the bar's name, NICKS LOUNGE. No apostrophe. Not sure why. The owner had painted the glass front door and scratched a rectangular peephole in the paint to be able to look out. Of course, people scratched their initials in the paint, as well as along the doorframe: *PEROS* and *GHOST* and a bunch of other illegible names and words.

I just can't comprehend someone thinking that shade of blue was a good choice no matter how cheap the paint must have been. And just for good measure, the walls inside are the same shade. Someone did have the sense to paint the wainscoting black. Nicks has carpet on the floors, so it always reeks of stinky feet and stale beer.

But despite it all, I love the place. I feel safe there. At home.

Walking back from the bar one night with Mr. Delbert, I asked him what he did to stay healthy.

He said, I haven't ever worked out in my life except for chasing my kids around the house. And now I just walk Mr. Dog.

I imagined his small frame, lean and sinewy, his slow and delicate footsteps, walking eighty-pound Mr. Dog.

That's something. He's huge, I said.

I wouldn't get no small-ass dog, Mr. Delbert said. What's the point? A small dog doesn't scare anybody, and it just irritates the shit out of you. Plus, you don't even need to walk a little dog. Mr. Dog, he keeps me honest. I have to walk him every morning.

I said, Mr. Dog scares my daughter. She's nicknamed him *Monster*.

Mr. Delbert smiled and said, I like that. But if you want the truth, Mr. Dog is just a big sweetheart. You'd be surprised how many big dogs are nothing but little babies on the inside.

Mr. Delbert opened the chain-link gate to his yard. Mr. Dog paced back and forth, waiting for him to come in. He barked at me. Mr. Delbert grabbed Mr. Dog's jowls, tugging hard from the left to the right, whispering, *Are you a monster? Are you a monster?*

Since I definitely was not planning on getting a big-ass dog, I figured I'd ask some of the other men in my life what they're doing to maintain their vim, their vigor.

My lover/boyfriend/weekly houseguest Jared said, Absolutely nothing and neither should you. I like big bellies.

He reached over and rubbed mine. Somehow, this bothered me. Actually, everything about my situation with him bothered me, because I'm fucked up. Like we've been seeing each other for about six months, and things are going smoothly between us, so clearly something must be wrong, clearly this can't be a good thing. He's smart, a bit round and stocky like me, and generally well dressed, unlike me. His hair and beard are always cleanly lined up, and his smile just plain sexy and cocky. Like he's about to say, Yes, you would totally enjoy doing just about anything with me. Even exercising.

I can't help but desire him and want to prove him wrong at the same time.

So after he said that I went to work out twice in one week.

When I told Bob the Bartender I had started working out, he immediately asked, What do you do when you go to the gym?

I said, Some light weights, and then I spin on a stationary bike.

3

Bob the Bartender stopped wiping the counter and looked at me all serious. He is tall, slightly goofy in that lumbering, gangly young man sort of way. He always wears black pants, a black apron, and a white button-up shirt with a black bow tie. I have never seen him in anything else. He asked, Do you wear spandex?

I said, I do, but.

I knew it, he interrupted, You totally wear spandex. You do.

I just nodded and said, Yes. Yes, I do.

He walked away glowing like I made his night.

Sitting with me at the bar was Jason. We're best friends even though he's an old crusty punk who bikes in cut-off black denim shorts, on a bike adorned with political stickers and a milk crate. Plus he's got fine blondish-brown hair and skin scarred by child-hood acne. Not my type. Our friendship happened slowly over time and alcohol and bad lighting in our bar.

When I asked Jason how he stayed in shape, he said, That's why I don't have a car. It makes me have to bike everywhere. Look at these.

He proceeded to roll up the black denim shorts above his shock-ingly hairless and muscular thighs. He left his shorts that way for the rest of the evening, bragging to the Thursday night regulars and various customers about his self-described *biker legs*.

It was my daughter, Stella, who broke the once-a-month workout morass I found myself in. She's in her senior year of high school and embodies the profoundly powerful stubbornness of teenage women everywhere. I can do no right. Her mother Betsy and I share her week to week, and by the end of each week we are so happy to pass her off, we smile and wink to each other as we hug Stella goodbye. It's coparenting at its finest.

Stella and I had just eaten a pepperoni pizza because I didn't feel like cooking and she always complains about my cooking anyway. Plus the last time I made dinner we bickered over the fact that I tend to make the same few meals over and over. I'm a creature of habit. I don't like change.

Dad, there's more to Italian food than pasta and red sauce, she said.

Right. There's meatballs, I said, stabbing one with my fork.

You just don't get it, she said as if that *just* explained her position precisely.

What exactly don't I get? I hand-rolled the meat and added the spices. You used to love doing that with me. In fact, Ms. Healthy, you used to try and eat the raw meatballs when I wasn't looking.

We stared at each other for a second. She looked like she might throw a meatball at me.

She said, What I mean is that there are a variety of sauces besides red sauce.

Name some, I dared her.

There's pesto. There's cacio e pepe. There's creamy garlic sauces. Even bean and nut sauces.

There's that orange one like from mac-and-cheese boxes, I teased.

Stop, Dad. Just stop. How about you try something new, and then I will be excited to eat your pasta again. She stood up and walked to her room.

That night I finished the meatballs angry and alone, and since then, when we're having dinner together, I usually just order out: Thai, Ethiopian, or pizza.

So we were eating pizza when she told me that her biology class assignment was to measure and weigh different human bodies and compare body mass index across gender and age lines.

Dad, she said, I need to measure your body for my class.

Absolutely not, I said, adjusting my posture a bit and pushing the pizza box away.

Dad, she said. Seriously. I need to do this. I need to get an A. Don't you want to support my education?

Her hand on her hip. Her face crumpled in reproach. Her long hair pulled up in a bun that punctuated the top of her head. She said it like her acceptance to college depended on my participation. She said it like I've failed her for most of her life.

Fine, I said.

I stood up and walked from the table in the kitchen to the tiny living room, which housed my work desk along one wall and one bookshelf and small couch along the other wall. Though it was a cool September evening, the room was boiling because the heater only had one setting: super high. Wrapping the yellow fabric tape across my forehead, she measured my skull.

Big, huh? I said.

Average, she responded.

She measured my chest, saying, Breathe in and out.

I did again and again and again. Like I would never stop.

Next, my arm span. She gripped the tip of my finger on my left hand and asked me to hold the end of the tape measure, and she then stepped to the other side of me.

I felt infinite. She continued to measure. The distance between my armpit and waist. The distance between my hip and foot. She had a look on her face. Intense. Driven. Beautiful. I felt myself expand.

I asked, Do you remember when I used to ask if you knew how much I loved you, and you'd say *this much* and measure a few inches with your fingers, and then I'd say *even more,* and you'd measure maybe a foot with your hands, and I'd say *nope, it's even more than that,* and you'd measure out farther and farther and until you couldn't possibly stretch any more.

Hold still, Dad, she said.

I couldn't. I dropped my arms. I needed her to hear me. I needed to know she remembered.

Do you? I asked.

She looked at me and said, Of course I do, and then she hugged me and put her head to my chest. She said, I hear your heart.

What's it sound like?

Like you're alive.

When she got to the circumference of my belly, she actually laughed out loud.

What? I asked.

Nothing.

What, I demanded, raising my voice.

Well, she said and wrote something down in her notebook. Then as if proving a hypothesis she announced, You're disproportionate.

How am I disproportionate? I asked.

Your head and chest and stomach. You better do something if you want to live a long, healthy life. She walked away, her bun bouncing with each step. The room empty of sound except for the heater blasting away.

From that point on, I changed my behavior. I'm doing something. Of course, I want to live a long, healthy life. For the last couple months, on my drinking Tuesdays and Thursdays, the nights I allow myself to go to Nicks, I buy bitters and soda for the first hour and then drink one shot of Bulleit over the second hour as I sit making small talk with Jason and Mr. Delbert, watching the basketball game or sports highlights.

I bike instead of drive to do my errands, smiling as I think of Jason's thighs. When I slip on my black-and-neon-orange spandex shorts that match my black-and-neon-orange spandex top, I smirk thinking about what Bob the Bartender would say if he saw me.

I feel good, but my belly refuses to retreat. I wonder if it's genetic. I rub it and feel the muscles under the skin, the fat, the jolly bounce and shake of it.

Today, after I finished a project revamping a restaurant's website, I decided to go biking for exercise and pleasure. I shut my laptop and grabbed my bike, an expensive red and black Bianchi Vigorelli I purchased used off of Craigslist. I flew out of my apartment and pedaled up to the corner of my street and King, where Mr. Delbert lived. I howled at Mr. Dog. For once the dog didn't rush the fence as I passed, but continued to sit at the front door of Mr. Delbert's house. I sped down King over the speed bumps, past the fixed-up Victorian houses alongside old, rundown apartment buildings like mine, under the massive oak trees that are beginning to litter the street with their crunchy, dry leaves as fall approaches.

I biked to the shoreline, biked past cars stuck on the freeway, biked past Golden Gate Fields. I heard the flap of my windbreaker. I blended in with the other riders in matching spandex outfits. I stared at the thighs of the men and women and appreciated the androgyny of it all. I imagined measuring each person, instructing them to move and bend, to stretch their bodies wider and wider.

Heading back home, I felt alive and even happy to face my vegetarian dinner and my daughter, and that's when I rolled up on the emergency lights and Mr. Dog stuck in a cage.

I walk to the animal control truck and look at the animal, muzzled and slobbery.

I say to the woman in uniform, Can I take him?

The fire truck pulls away, and she's now the only official left.

Please, I say.

Can you control him? she asks.

Of course, I lie.

She looks to see if anybody is watching, then says, Then take him quickly. I don't want to have to do all the paperwork, anyway.

I turn to the dog locked up in the kennel on the truck. I have never petted him without Mr. Delbert standing right there. I usually just bark or howl or yell Hello when I rush by the house.

Now I coo, Hey there, Mr. Dog. You're ok. You're ok. I repeat this like a lullaby or a prayer. I reach in blindly, knowing it's the dumbest thing I could possibly do. I take off the muzzle and grab his collar. I pull him free. He bounds out immediately and sits beside me. I stare at him for a second, at his heavy breathing and lips covered in drool and big eyes looking back at me. I lead him and my bike back to my apartment, and he heels like I've walked him every morning.

Later, my daughter and I feed him some bacon, the only meat I have in the kitchen because I'm trying not to eat too much of it. I'm trying to stay healthy, to live long. With a few towels, I make him a place to sleep on the floor in my room. Sometime in the middle of the night, Mr. Dog sneaks into my bed. I wake to see his looming figure blotting the light from the streetlamp outside my window. I watch him try and get comfortable, circling and circling. Eventually, he simply falls onto me, heavy and warm, his head in the curve of my armpit.

I know I should shoo him off the bed, but I pet him, and he stretches out wide. I wonder how long he is. The distance between paw and chest, between head and tail. I wonder if he's disproportionate, as well. He doesn't seem to mind the way my belly fits against his body. I wonder if he's worried, if he feels loss, how much he misses Mr. Delbert. I put my hand on his chest and feel his heart. It beats in steady, constant thumps, like he's answering me: *this much, this much, this much.*

2

The Opposite of Human

Stella left her underwear on the bathroom floor again. There they are staring at me in the muted yellow light. This red lacy thong, all balled up.

The fact that they are there, on the floor, definitely bothers me. Because this isn't the first time it's happened. We've had talks about it. We've joked about it. I've even bitched about it, hating the sound of my own whiny voice as I yelled: Stella, get your undies off the floor.

They're called underwear, Dad. I'm not three. And sometimes you just have to make a quick exit, she'd said, like I should understand that choice.

I don't even know what that means, I responded. What would require running from the bathroom without your underwear?

She shrugged and added, Since when have you become so concerned about what the bathroom floor looks like? Is it because Jared is coming over? She raised her eyebrows like I was guilty of something.

I'd definitely become more fastidious since her mother and I divorced five years ago, amicably for the most part. I keep things clean, which is why I said no when Mr. Delbert's family asked if I wanted to keep Mr. Dog. I did, but I didn't want all the shedding and the shit that came with owning a dog.

And, yes, Jared, my boyfriend—though I hate that term—has been spending a night or two during the weeks Stella stays with me. And, yes, recently he sauntered back to the bedroom laughing. He joked about how I should clean up after having somebody over. I had no idea what he was talking about.

He said, The dirty panties in the bathroom. It's kind of uncouth, if you know what I mean.

I knew what he meant, of course.

But even more than them balled up on the floor, what really bothers me is the kind of underwear they are. Fuck-me panties. Sexy panties. Panties you put on for lovers.

So staring at the panties on the floor once again, I ponder my options.

I consider calling her mother and asking whether or not Stella does the same thing over there, but knowing Betsy, she'll take the question as an attack on her parenting choices, which might lead to an argument and a statement about how I can be such a selfish, blaming asshole sometimes. And I know it's true. Sometimes I can.

I consider putting the thong on my daughter's bed, but she wouldn't even see that I placed it on her pillow or her desk or her lampshade, for that matter, because she usually has clothes thrown all over everything.

I consider leaving them there till she returns from her mother's, and though that's four days of staring at them, I conclude that if I wait, I can pile on a little bit of shaming. I can say things like: *Please don't leave your dirty underwear on the floor so that anyone who uses the bathroom will see them. Aren't you embarrassed? Did your boyfriend buy them for you? Do you know what they say? What they mean?*

I smile and think, *Shame. That sounds just right.*

I walk out of the bathroom, leaving the panties for all to see, which over the course of the next four days will only be Jared. But still, I feel like a serious father teaching a serious lesson.

Tuesday and Wednesday and Thursday all pass as I tediously upgrade a client's website. They're calling the upgrade an *inauguration*, as if it were presidential. I get emails from them with words like *prognosis, functionality, user-ship, interactivity*, even the word *luminosity*. Words disconnected from the real world bother me as much as politics. I respond curtly.

Every time I go to the bathroom, I see the red lacy thong. It kills me not to reach down and pick it up, to just deal with it.

But I remind myself, every time, not to.

This is what they call a teaching opportunity. There's the principle, I remind myself. Manners are at stake. You just can't go around leaving your undies on bathroom floors. It's like peeing on the toilet seat.

It's Friday, and I'm grumpy. I drank a bit too much last night at Nicks.

Tuesdays and Thursdays I used to let myself go, imbibing what I wanted, all night long if I wanted. I enjoyed everything about those two days. Like Sabbaths. Like national holidays. But in my attempt to live a long life, I now drink sparkly water for the first beverage and then nurse my one bourbon. But last night Jason convinced me to order a beer back because it was such a classic thing to do. When we enlisted Bob the Bartender to explain how to properly word the request—bourbon, beer back or bourbon with a beer back—because somehow we felt this linguistic distinction important, he shared that no one ever orders a bourbon with a beer back at Nicks. We had to prove him wrong. A couple of times, unfortunately.

We also debated whether my daughter should go to the local community college or to a four-year college.

I said, Who needs debt? Because there's no way I can afford to pay the tuition, so she'd have to take out loans.

Fuck worrying about debt, Jason replied. I'm telling you by the time she needs to pay that shit back, the system will crash. So tell her not to stress and to take out them loans!

I shook my head at Jason's ridiculousness. The bar started to fill up with patrons, mostly neighborhood folks who have been coming to Nicks forever, just some men and a few women who came dressed up, like the carpet in the bar was red. Like the place was special. Frankie, who always seemed to be wearing the same clothes—a fancy suit, the kind with a handkerchief in the breast pocket, something clearly from the '70s—always ordered a tall gin and tonic with a slim black straw and a lemon wedge he'd squeeze into the beverage. Susan, the upstairs tenant, acted like the queen of the place, like if we pissed her off she could get us kicked out.

I hadn't yet taken Jared to Nicks. It's not that I wouldn't like him to meet my friend Jason or the various characters that fill my two nights a week at the bar, but I don't want some awkward coming-out party, and that's how it would feel.

I sat back in the chair next to Jason, missing Mr. Delbert's presence. The bar felt bereft without him. But I also felt strangely uncomfortable with this nostalgia for a person I barely knew. He'd told me he had kids. Two daughters. He described how kids used to run wild in our neighborhood—that there were so many you could trust all the other parents to watch out, to keep an eye on their behavior. He winked when he told me that other parents make the best cops. I knew his daughters had moved away to southern California, leaving him alone in his house with the perfectly square hedges under each picture window. I never asked what happened with his wife. I didn't know much of anything about him other than what included me: Mr. Dog and our banter over chain-link fences or beverages. I wonder if there might have been some wisdom I missed out on. Like how to discipline daughters or pay for college.

I had loved strolling by Mr. Delbert's house, how he often stood on his porch with Mr. Dog.

Every time I walked by, he'd say, Gonna be a good evening?

And I said every time in response, It already is.

He'd reply, You say that every time.

And I'd say, You have to start somewhere.

I'd then say, Hello, Mr. Dog.

The dog just ran along the fence growling, growling.

I was trying to imagine what Mr. Delbert would say about the college debate when Frankie, who sat on the other side of me and rarely spoke more than a few words, suddenly broke in, You know, neither one of you get it. It's really not about where to go or how much to pay. It's the leaving that's the point.

With that he sipped his gin and tonic through the black slim straw.

Jason said, True. I moved all the way to Sacramento after high school and drove back more often to go see shows at Gilman than to see my parents.

Are you trying to depress me? You think I'm that bad of a father? That she just wants to leave?

What you are or are not as a father probably has nothing to do with it, my friend, Jason said.

I nodded. Even Frankie nodded.

Hey. I leaned in close to Jason trying to keep the conversation just between us. So do you think it's weird that my daughter leaves her underwear on the bathroom floor?

She lives there, right? With you? Then you should be happy she does. That's a sign of comfort. I bet most fathers would love to have their daughters that comfortable with them.

Really? I asked.

He thought about it for a second and said, No. Most fathers are total chumps.

Chump's a good word, Frankie said.

Jason nodded again, in that self-assured way you do when you know you're right.

What else was there to say?

I bought them both drinks, and then another round for me and Jason.

Now I'm paying for it a second time with this hangover. All morning, I feign interest in the website's inauguration. At two, I give up and decide to play online Scrabble. I struggle with every group of letters I get. I can play only three-letter words: *pet, jog, saw*. I think of my daughter moving away.

Stella finally comes home from school. I can tell she's upset. Normally she says Hi, gives me a hug and a peck on the cheek, makes small talk for a few minutes, and then runs to her room to put on music so loud I feel like I'm part of a sitcom.

Today she walks into the kitchen while I stir my afternoon coffee.

She says, You're always just standing there when I come home. What do you do while I'm gone?

I work, I say. I clean up, I add, trying so hard not to immediately bring up the underwear.

She waits for more.

I ask, Is that really what you want to talk about? Is everything all right?

She switches her purse—one I don't recognize, an expensive looking leather satchel—from one shoulder to the other shoulder, and says, Why are guys such assholes?

She waits.

I shrug, unsure how to respond.

I say, Is this perhaps about the guy who bought you those Victoria's Secret–looking panties that you left on the bathroom floor for anyone to see?

She stares at me with such disdain I put down my cup of coffee.

I scrunch up my face at her, trying to lighten the mood.

She puts her hands to her face like she's trying not to cry. Then drops her purse on the ground and storms to the bathroom.

The contents of the purse spill out. Lined notebook papers and her makeup bag spread across the floor.

I want to answer her question, to tell her why guys are assholes, but how to explain? Because we weren't held enough as children. Because when the people we love leave, it hurts. Because our fathers and brothers and friends ridiculed us when we were anything but what they expected us to be. Because misogyny. Because patriarchy. Because fear. Because self-loathing. Because we were taught to be strong rather than kind. Because feelings are as useless as a flaccid cock. Because no one ever says be a human. They say be a man, meaning the exact opposite of human.

But I say nothing. Instead, I yell to her to come back to the kitchen.

When she does, I say, Please pick up your purse. It spilled.

She goes to the purse and bends over, and I see the underwear she's wearing, black and lacy.

She gathers her stuff and walks to her room. She doesn't look back. She doesn't say a word. Not a single thing. I pick up my mug and sip my coffee. I walk to the bathroom. I see the underwear. Still there. Just where she left them four days ago.

I finally reach down and pick them up and walk to the laundry basket by the washer. I shuffle the clothes around and bury the panties in with the other dirty laundry as if they were always there.

I don't bring it up again, and when she leaves to go to her mother's the following week, it's not panties on the floor, it's two bowls of half-eaten granola with almond milk. She brought them from her room, and instead of putting them in the sink, let alone washing the bowls, she leaves them on the counter for me to deal with.

Betsy and I talk a few days later, and when I tell her about Stella's brazen disregard for cleanliness, Betsy reminds me that Stella is very stressed with her SAT preparation.

I know, I say. But I don't know. And I feel left out of something by not knowing.

Betsy tries to commiserate, but I'm too irritated to participate. She tells me I should not be too mean with Stella despite how hard it might be and that, yes, Stella is just as messy at her place.

I promise to help Stella and to cut her some slack, which in my mind means making sure she eats dinner before she hides in her room doing whatever it is she does in there. I start asking if she needs any help, and when she acts put out with me for asking, I feel less guilty about doing my own thing once she retreats to her room, like going to Nicks or meeting up with Jared to see a movie. I never see her Fridays or Saturdays because she always has plans. In fact, she even encourages me to go out in that completely transparent way teenagers have of trying to get you out of their space.

Perhaps it's time you mosey on up the street, Dad, she said last Thursday when I tried to help her read up on various colleges.

I'm not dumb. I knew it was a ploy. But I took her up on it.

Tonight in the bar it's just me and Bob the Bartender, who has recently claimed to be a poet. I've never asked to see his writing, and he's never offered.

When I enter, he says, Juan Gutiérrez.

And I say, Bob the Bartender.

We nod, and he busies himself doing what bartenders do when there's absolutely no one in a bar and they want to avoid chatting. I realize as I wait for Jason, who always shows up around nine, that I've known Bob the Bartender for a couple years now. I wonder what he knows about me besides my exercise routine and attire. I wonder if he'd miss me if I stopped coming to Nicks. If I disappeared.

He slides the remote down the bar and then a sparkly water. Soon he will come over with my tumbler of Bulleit. It's decent bourbon, and if I'm going to pay six dollars for a shot, I might as well pay eight and get quality. I deserve it, I tell myself. I do.

My daughter, earlier in the afternoon, reminded me not to

spend too much, that I needed to put away the amount I promised for her college tuition.

I reminded her to wash her dishes left on the counter.

She said, That's a straw-man argument, Dad.

I corrected her, It's a red herring.

Either way, she said, fallacious.

She hugged me, patted my back, and said Godspeed as Betsy pulled up.

Because of her SAT cramming, she's using words that never sound right in a sentence spoken by anyone whose first language is English. Like effulgence and fecund and Godspeed.

She marched to the car, arrogant, confident like a cop, then waved to me from the backseat. Not waving back, I watched them drive away, taillights blinking as the car hit speed bump after speed bump.

Bob eventually asks, The same?

Yes.

He grabs a glass and the bottle of Bulleit.

The ice cubes seem to sparkle, and the bourbon looks warm and inviting—perfect for this October evening in Oakland. Somehow even the horrid blue walls glow with energy.

I sip, and the burn wakes me up. I ask Bob, Did you take the SAT?

Yes, he says, and the GRE.

Really?

Yes, he says. And I did well on both.

His girlfriend walks in—blond, slim—and unwraps her scarf, and gets stuck for a second fumbling with the material around her throat. I fight the urge to think of her paternally.

Hi, she says and sits on the stool next to me.

This place stinks, she says.

I agree, I say.

Bob says, I agree too.

There's a silence like we all just expressed something profound.

Then I ask, Bob, did the test help you in any part of your real life?

I probably could solve a basic math question, he says, placing a gin and tonic in front of his girlfriend, who's folding the scarf into a perfect square.

She says, I love taking tests. She says it like someone looking for a hug.

We both turn to her.

Rachel, Bob says, no one was really talking to you.

I can't tell if Bob is being serious or not. His face reveals nothing. I figure she must be able to read it. I look up at the screen showing the Warriors game. The TV is boxy and bulky, something from the mid-'90s, precariously hung in the corner, backlighting Bob in that comforting cathode light. I hear Rachel snap something back to Bob. They bark on, and I watch the ball being dribbled, reach into my pocket and finger the two twenty dollar bills.

I sip the bourbon, still warm and welcoming. *Godspeed,* I think to myself.

Bob and Rachel, I say loudly so they have to take notice. How many words do you think there are for goodbye?

Bob says, I have no idea.

Rachel says, So long. Farewell. Toodle-oo. Adiós.

In English, I say.

She says, Don't you think adiós is anglicized by now? Just like arrivederci. Bon voyage. Ciao. See, I told you I'm good at tests.

Sayonara, Bob says in a fake accent and bows.

Don't be a racist asshole, Rachel says.

Bob the Bartender saunters away like he's got something important to do

I lean into Rachel, Why do you think men are assholes?

Because they're men.

I purse my lips and say, That's a logical fallacy.

And there's your answer. Mansplaining, for one thing.

But. Wait. Did you set me up for that?

Is that a rhetorical question?

No. I think it's a real question?

Are you implying something about women and their wily, wily ways?

Absolutely not, I say and sip my beverage, looking around for Bob, envious of his stealthy departure. She shoves me.

Man, relax. I'm fucking with you. She laughs. She puts her hand over her lips and then back to her drink. Men, she says. Assholes and so gullible.

I check my watch, a silver Seiko, the only thing I still own from my father. And he was, in fact, an asshole. I wonder where Jason is. I spin my chair in circles and watch as the bar starts to fill. Besides me and Frankie and Susan from Upstairs, the bar also gets a younger crowd, partly because Mondays, Wednesdays, and weekends the owner hosts events, karaoke, djs, and a poetry open mic, which I would never go to. I'm happy to have Tuesdays and Thursdays with nothing going on but drinking.

Jason bursts in and, seeing the Warriors racing up and down the court, yells, Yes. Game's still on! Jason is earnest and politically correct about everything that comes up, but he also loves to talk professional sports. He sits and greets Frankie and Susan from Upstairs. He may not be the most graceful guy, but he certainly is respectful.

Jason, I ask him, Why do you think men are such assholes? Asking for my daughter. Rachel here says because they're men.

I defer to her. Jason faux bows and adds, Hello, Rachel.

I say, My daughter would point out that that's some type of fallacious argument. I can't remember which.

Jason says, Let's tease it out. Men are assholes because of patriarchy, which negatively impacts their relationships with children and women and other men, so Rachel is absolutely right. Men are assholes because of men, i.e., the patriarchy.

Bam, she yells, and they high-five.

I say, Isn't that another form of mansplaining?

Rachel says, If I agree with the mansplanation then it's not mansplaining.

I say, I'm so confused.

Just trust me, Rachel says, and we all clink our glasses.

Bob the Bartender gets busy. Rachel gets tipsy and cocky and starts solving a math problem on a paper napkin to further demonstrate her test-taking capabilities. I drink through my first twenty. Frankie stoically sits at the curve of the bar. As I break the next twenty, I think of the money I'm trying to save to help my daughter leave. We have to learn to say goodbye to so many things. Hasta la vista. Au revoir. I think of all the people and all the things I've had to let go of. I watch people come into the bar and the way they greet each other. I watch when they leave. I listen to the words they use as they hug and walk away from each other. I imagine my daughter. I wish I had waved back to her.

When Stella does graduate and most likely leaves for some college far away, I will already know the feeling of goodbye. It's words that never really feel comfortable in your mouth. It's ugly blue walls you grow to love. It's panties on the floor. It's people who become your friends despite everything.

3

The Difference between Fronting and Lying

Seriously, Dad. You have to do the FAFSA. Like tonight. I need the info for my applications.

Seriously, Stella. Why did you wait until the night before it's due to remind me? You know this is not very adult of you.

We are squared off by the small table that serves as both desk and dinner table. I had just stepped out of the shower and was prepping for a dinner date with Jared when I was confronted by an angry daughter.

Dad. You're the parent. You're the one who should've known about this shit. I'm the teenager, and it's my responsibility?

Oh, so now you're a teenager?

I can see Stella is about to run to her room. I realize I need to be the good guy. I need to help her without giving her a hard time. A difficult thing, indeed.

Fine. Give me a few minutes. I need to get dressed and then I guess cancel my plans with Jared. I'm also going to call your mother.

I'm not sure why, but when I say this it comes out like threat.

Good. You guys never talk. Maybe if you did, this wouldn't happen.

And like a practiced dancer, she pirouettes and storms away. She leaves her bowl of granola and a half-eaten apple on the table. I have to clear it to make space for my laptop.

Why are you always eating granola at seven at night, I yell, knowing she won't hear it because of the music bumping from her room. I step outside and walk down the steps to the building's front lawn, brown and mottled and in need of maintenance.

I phone Jared, who prefers calls to texts, he told me one night after sex when I was all malleable. He said, We've been dating long enough, Juan. Pick up the damn phone and call your boy when you need to say something. I mean a cute text is fine and all, but a phone call. That's commitment.

He said this while rubbing my belly.

How could I resist, despite the word *commitment*?

His phone rings as I look up the street. Mr. Delbert's house dark and abandoned. Sad and lonely. A FOR SALE sign went up soon after he died, and every weekend for a month afterward the street was flooded with a shocking number of freshly washed cars, sedans with anxious-looking young couples double parking, car locks beeping as they ran into the open house.

I wanted to be angry or irritated, especially when one young man asked me about the neighborhood.

Meaning what, I asked?

Meaning is it safe? He asked.

I cocked my head, annoyed to find myself in a conversation supposedly about one thing but really about another thing.

But how could I hate on him when I had been just like him, meaning I moved to this neighborhood with Betsy and little baby Stella, excited and nervous to make a home, not knowing anything about the area other than it was affordable. We rented an apartment in one of the few scattered buildings in a neighborhood of mostly houses, nicely renovated Victorians and that '50s block style like Mr. Delbert's.

When I think about it now, I realize I'm envious of the young man. Because we didn't buy. Because no one I knew bought. Because my parents never considered it. Jason would say something about housing racism. Jared would probably agree.

I told the young man that the neighborhood wasn't safe and walked up the stairs of my unmaintained apartment building painted a flat brown.

Jared answers, and I say, Hey, I have to cancel tonight. Need to help Stella with a financial aid application.

Ouch. That can't be fun.

It won't be. I promise you.

Juan, I do want to say I wish you'd let me know in advance. Especially since you're not inviting me over to join in the fun.

You'd want to come over and help?

No. I'd want to come over to see you. And I like Stella. I like watching you get shit from her. Maybe I'll mention something about panties on the floor.

Don't you dare.

He chuckles. Are you a wee bit nervous?

I'll show you how nervous I am later.

Promises, promises, he says, but then lowers his voice into that serious tone and warns, But don't you dare call me *your friend* like last time. I'm telling you now to call me your boyfriend. If you can't say that to Stella, then forget it. You and your taxes and your raging teen daughter can fend for yourselves.

Fine. But bring pizza.

That means I have to drive and not bike. Damn, you're pushing it.

I then text Betsy: Why didn't you take care of the FAFSA with Stella? I inserted a shit emoji to show that I'm mad but not too mad. I want to blame her. I want to tell her she has to come over right now and deal with it. The phone buzzes.

Hi, I answer.

Hello, Juan, Betsy says. So just an FYI, I did sit with her this week and go over my tax info. Though remember if you're claiming her then the bulk of that info needs to come from you. And I should add I helped her with her application essay, which if you haven't read, you should. I think it's super interesting. Maybe even telling.

I feel defensive, like she's trying to rile me or give a back-handed *I told you so*. Of course, the fact that Stella hadn't asked me to look at her essay stings as well.

I lie and say, I know about the essay. We're going to talk about it tonight.

Feeling scolded now by both Jared and Betsy, I hang up.

Even from the lawn I can hear the music from Stella's room, a soft pulse.

I text Jared: And wine. Then I text again: Please and thank you. Jared replies with an ok emoji and a slice of cake emoji.

Upstairs, I clear the table. I decide to put some music on, something soft and romantic, and find a Nina Simone station. "Break Down and Let It All Out" begins.

I start the parental portion of the FAFSA application and feel myself get into a rhythm like I do at work. Almost an hour has flown by when Stella comes to the table. She's changed into sweatpants and a bro shirt that reveals the sides of her torso. She isn't wearing a bra. I struggle for a second, trying to figure out how to comment on her attire without commenting on her attire.

I say, Jared is bringing pizza and wine. I realize I should have checked in with you. Are you cool with him coming over?

Dad, you're the only one who is all awkward.

I shrug. Well, you might be too when I begin to meet the people you date.

How do you know I'm not dating someone? She asks.

I look at her. She's sitting with her arms crossed and her long hair tied up in a bun.

Are you all right? I pull my hands away from the keyboard and shift to face her. She stares like she's trying to figure out how to respond. She slumps her shoulders.

I'm just stressed about all this stuff. There's a lot to do, you know. Maybe you don't remember.

I do, but I have to ask, Are you seeing someone?

Dad, no. Really? That's what you just heard.

No. I just. I guess I'm feeling like there's a lot of little things I don't know about you anymore.

She shakes her head like she's not sure what to say.

The doorbell rings. Neither of us moves.

She says, Aren't you gonna get that?

How do you know it's for me?

Only old people use doorbells?

What does that mean?

My friends would just text that they're here.

Your friends are hella dumb, I say.

When I open the door, Jared swoops in holding a pizza from the worker-owned collective Cheeseboard Pizza and a box of cheap wine. He always dresses so fine. So colorful. Or not colorful, but always coordinated with just the right splash of color. Tonight it's a fresh light-purple sweater, fancy denim jeans, and black dress shoes.

I feel disheveled in old Levis, my house slippers, and a t-shirt. But I'm freshly shaved, so I hope that makes up for something.

A box? I ask, a bit aghast.

He cocks his head. You talking about the pizza or the wine? He leans in, and I kiss him on the lips.

We sit around the table. I keep side-eying Stella to see if she registers anything about Jared and me. She has finished a slice and poured herself a glass of wine. We all have a glass in front of us.

Perhaps I need to get you some wine glasses, Jared says.

What's the problem with these glasses?

One mason jar and two...what are these?

Moroccan tea glasses, Stella says.

They're pretty, but...Jared leaves his meaning for us to infer.

Stella laughs. She sounds deeply happy. I try to remember the last time I heard her sound like that. I watch the way she moves the glass of wine to her mouth and back down. I feel something lovely and scary. Something I have no word for.

Are you drunk? Teenagers aren't what they used to be, I say.

Stella ignores me and says to Jared, You should get some boyfriend award for coming over.

Jared looks at me like he's impressed I set the record straight, that I must've talked with her about him being my boyfriend.

I say, Mom said something about your application essay? It being interesting? Want to talk about it with me? I don't have to read it if that makes you uncomfortable.

I was gonna talk to you about it. But I don't want you to be offended or anything.

What did you write about?

She sits up and puts her wine down. She's clearly practiced what she's going to say. She looks at Jared. Then at me. It feels conspiratorial. I nod, like what you share with me, you can share with him.

It's a response to that generic question: *tell us something that makes you special.*

Jared says, Like if you're a recovering addict or an orphan.

Right, Stella says.

A bit obvious don't you think, I say. How about your interest in biology and your skill at soccer.

That's great if she wants to go to Laney, Jared says.

What's wrong with Laney? It'd be cheaper. And she'd have a place to stay.

Dad, I'm right here. And I'm not going to Laney, and even if I did, I'd get my own place.

Jared says, In my opinion, if you all want to hear it...

I nod. Stella says, Yes, please.

Now's not the time to worry about money. It's time to imagine possibilities. Apply everywhere, Jared says like he's selling something. He reminds me of Jason at the bar talking politics. Or Frankie dispensing old man wisdom, cocksure and unwavering.

Stella says, Thank you, Jared. I wrote about being the child of teen parents. About Dad and Mom.

I'm not sure what to say, so I ask, What's the point of the piece? That teens should or shouldn't have kids?

Neither. The point is the perspective it gave me, Stella says in this flat way that makes me feel something like worry or regret.

What perspective is that?

I tried to imagine what it would be like to be a teen parent today. I tried to show how I learned things like empathy and nonconformity and patience.

Patience with us? Me and your mother? I ask a bit too defensively.

She says, You have to be a little cavalier to have kids at eighteen. I can't imagine having a child right now.

Probably a good thing, Jared whispers loudly.

Cavalier. That's an SAT word for sure, I say.

I see Jared sipping red wine, smirking.

Why not write about being Chicanx? I ask. I know I'm showing off a bit, and my daughter nods in approval, but I can only imagine my father hearing that word, so it doesn't yet feel right to say aloud.

Because I'm not. Not really.

How're you not really? You're half.

I'm half white too.

Jared adds, Obama's half white. But he's black. Period, right?

But I don't really fit in with the other Latinx students at my school. I can't speak Spanish. I feel like my roots are something I learned about in a book.

Eso es la culpa de tu papi, chica. Puedes practicar conmigo, Jared says.

Shut up, I say, eyeballing him.

Dad, what could I say? I'm a pocha. A mixed-race white girl. A product of American colonialism and cultural amnesia. I feel like I'm faking it.

Damn, Jared says. Yes. Say exactly that. But to be honest, and this is a bit of honesty from one symbolic pocho to another, we're all fronting a little bit. We all are learning about who we want to be and who we are. The difference lies between fronting and lying. Especially to ourselves. You can't front on yourself.

I want to get off this subject quickly. Speaking Spanish and family.

So you wrote about me and your mom. What did you say?

I'm stuck, actually. Because I feel like I don't know anything about you guys as young parents.

I try not to sound irritated when I say, Honey, how about you ask some questions then?

Stella immediately sits more upright and opens her laptop.

She asks, How did you and Mom even fall in love?

Falling in love is easy, I say. Staying in love is the work. And I still love your mother. I do. We just needed something else. Something different. I don't know how else to explain it.

Obviously. Like you needed to see men. She gestures in this game-show kind of way to Jared, who in a game-show kind of way bows.

I look at her. Like she said something vulgar. She looks back at me. Like *don't you try to deny it.*

Yes, that was some of it, but not all. Your mom knew about me and men.

Ok. Stop.

No, I say loudly, a bit too sharply. I wasn't really angry. Irritated, for sure. But something in me feels hot and urgent.

I say, You want to know about me? About your mother? Then you have to learn to listen to the whole story. You have to see your parents as people too. Like you. As hard as that is.

Did you do that with your parents? she jabs back.

No. It was easier to walk away from all that, which is something I certainly hope you're not planning on doing.

She stares silently at me.

I wait. I breathe in. I let the moment sit. I know the feeling now pulsing through my body. Fear. Guilt.

I say, And if I'm being honest, maybe me running away was part of why your mom and I didn't stay together. Too much shit we both never dealt with. Instead, we jumped headlong into each other. And that was beautiful.

Stella's face reminds me of her mother's. Her skin color, darker, like mine—but that smile, those eyes.

I feel Jared watching me. I don't look at him.

I say, I remember in the beginning we shared that apartment off Durant. We owned nothing. We had no furniture but this futon cushion. No frame even. And a big ass TV. We started to line the living room with empty wine bottles that we drank. We chose the date we finished lining the whole room as the date we'd marry in the future. October 26. Those might have been the best four months of our relationship.

What happened?

We graduated, and you came.

That feels shitty, she says.

Jared fills up our glasses.

Sorry. What I meant to say was that our daily life changed. Graduation. Jobs. New interests.

I reach out to touch her. I say, But you coming was the best thing we ever did. The best decision of my life.

I can feel myself choking up and getting angry about it at the same time. I don't want to cry. I don't. Jared touches my back. Stella watches this. I feel exposed.

I continue, But that apartment. All that cheap wine. Those months. We just reveled in each other. It was … something close to beauty.

I finally look at Jared.

That's a good story, he says.

Stella nods and says, I have an idea now. I'm gonna go to my room. Write it up.

She stands and grabs her wine and tops it off.

Hey, I say.

Wine makes everything beautiful? Just like you said. Thank you, Dad, she says, and she walks calmly away.

That's not what I meant, I yell after her, but I feel my face break open in a smile.

Jared and I sit in silence. The music's been playing. It's some blues song.

I say, What was all that *don't lie to yourself* stuff? I can't help but smirk as I chide him a bit.

Deep, huh? That's some Nina Simone shit. That's right. Don't think I didn't notice the station, he says and sips his wine loudly.

You're a fool. I begin laughing, and Jared laughs with me. He opens his mouth wide, and his white teeth are stained a purple shockingly close to the hue of his sweater. I can't help it. I laugh even more. Harder, with complete abandon.

4

The Way Other People See You

We fucked up. And Stella is livid. With me. With Betsy. With the entire state of California. The kind of anger that resides in your mouth, coating every word you say. The kind of anger that has your whole body clenched like a fist. The kind of anger that has you on the verge of tears constantly. Not tears of release, but of frustration. She is all bitter words and balled-up body and teenage attitude. Stella is horrible to be around, looking at me with such contempt and ferocity. Scary the temper manifested by young people. Though perhaps it's understandable. What in their life do they have control over, really?

Betsy called to tell me the news. Calls from her are the only ones I answer, besides Jared, of course, since he guilted me into it.

Juan. We need to talk for a few minutes. Are you free? It's important.

I'd just come back from the grocery store and stood at the foot of the stairs to my apartment, holding two tote bags of mostly veggies —carrots and broccoli and kale greens poking over the top. There are six units in my building, and when we moved in, most were filled with other parents and kids. The patch of grass in the front was strewn with various broken-down toys. But over the last few years, because of rent hikes and new ownership, more single tenants have moved in, which means more building upkeep because they complain more. Fewer toys greet me as I come home. Someone just started a garden box with baby kale seedlings, erect and arrogant, staring up at me.

I felt good because I picked up a new project that would pay good money with not a lot of work other than the busy and repetitive kind, something I could say took longer than it actually did so I'd get a couple weeks off. Plus it was Thursday, and I had decided to drink a beer tonight with Jason. A little celebration.

I'm free. What's going on? I asked as I leaned my bike against the rail and sat at the foot of the stairs.

So apparently we both needed to file some form since we share custody. Plus Stella forgot to submit official transcripts.

You've got to be kidding.

I stood up and walked back and forth on the sidewalk. Right then Jason peddled by, no shirt, no helmet, waving both hands in the air, slapping his thighs and yelling: See you tonight, JG! I watched him bike on down the street, wondering which building he lived in. JG was the new nickname he'd given me after I shared with him my disappointment over never having one in childhood.

Are you ready for this? Betsy's voice pulled me back to our conversation.

Tell me.

She was denied admission to the UC system, which means to all the UC schools, and encouraged to reapply as a transfer student.

The first thing I thought of was all that work Stella had forced me to do. Then I corrected myself. All the work *she* had to do. I wanted also to be mad at Betsy for not knowing about the form. I corrected myself again. I should've known as well.

I asked, How'd Stella overlook the transcripts?

Betsy said, How'd we overlook them? We helped her how many times?

But not on transcript stuff, I almost yelled.

Juan! I'm just as angry at her and just so sad for her. But we need to be on her side right now, both of us.

I paced the sidewalk. There was no blaming someone else. I knew she was right, but I had this overwhelming desire to fight on principle. Because I wanted to be angry. Because I felt guilty. Because I failed my daughter. Just like she knew I would.

We decide to have a family emergency meeting the next night, which gives me time to think and get that drink.

I decide to call Jared.

You're joking, he says when I tell him. Are you ok?

I'm fine. She's going to be so incredibly pissed off, and I'm not going to want to be around her at all.

Juan, you sound upset. It's ok to have feelings about this. I can't imagine the pressure you are under to not screw up.

I didn't screw up.

I know. I was just saying. Let me begin again. Juan, do you need something from me? How can I help you?

No. I guess not. You're not even involved, to be honest.

There is a long silence. I know I said something to hurt him. I know he is sensitive about family and roles and labels.

Jared asks, What do you think my involvement is? Tell me, what would you say's my job description? His tone is scathing and sarcastic.

Jared. I'm sorry. You're right. I guess I'm just feeling...

He says nothing, waiting for me to trip through what I want to express.

... feeling angry or disappointed.

We speak for another few minutes, and he listens and asks questions and I move from pacing the sidewalk to calmly sitting back on the front step, spent and relieved. I breathe out and feel something close to gratitude for Jared. I thank him for being patient with me.

Jared says, Thank you for sharing your feelings with me, Juan. I love you.

We've just started saying *I love you*. He says it in this particular way. Stella might use the word *glib* to describe it. When I say it back to him, it's like something heavy is in my mouth. Not that I don't love him. I do. I think. But something else. I feel like the phrase means something more than *I love you*, something unspoken and large. But then I imagine him in his crisp white undershirt. His perfectly trimmed and lined-up beard. His hungry mouth. His soft, moisturized hands and forearms. My hands always smelled of pine and aloe for hours after touching him.

It turns out not to be a family meeting. It is an announcement. A proclamation. Stella, standing over me and Betsy as we sit on Betsy's ultramodern couch holding handmade clay tea cups, informs us that she will do her best to fight the decision, but she has decided to move to LA and attend Santa Monica Community College as she works to transfer to UCLA, her dream school. I wonder what we look like to her, sitting there mired in our own feelings—both excited and sad for her.

She says that she will need our support to get through the rest of her final semester and our help planning the move to LA. She doesn't want our opinions nor our fears dumped on her. She looks at us like we are bosses or cops. Not like we are her parents. Something bothers me, but I can't place it.

She thanks us and walks to her room.

I look at Betsy.

She says, I don't see any other option than to do what she wants.

I say, Until she sees we want the best for her. That we want to support her.

Right, and then we can express our concerns.

We clink our tea cups like conspirators.

The most difficult thing was that, despite her disappointment, Stella still had to maintain her grades, so I made it a point to call her every day she wasn't with me. Like tonight.

She picks up after one ring.

I ask her how the paper is going, the one she has to write for her poli-sci class on same-sex marriage.

She says, It's horrible. I can't find anything more to say than *duh*.

Well, you have to say more than *duh* to get a good grade.

She says, Yes. I know. Thanks.

I say, You should write something about fairness or something about equality.

She says, I'd rather write a paper opposing any marriage at all.

I say nothing because I feel like she is implying something.

Finally I ask, Why? Marriage is fine.

It is? She asks. Tell me, did you get married because you really wanted to or because you thought you had to.

At the time, I really wanted to, I say, but something doesn't feel right in my own response, and even I can hear it.

And if you hadn't married Mom, would you still have loved her?

Yes.

Then what more did you need? What did you gain by marrying her?

I guess nothing, I say.

She says, Except hefty fees when you got divorced. That's what I remember. You both yelling at each other about money.

That's what you remember? I ask. Do you remember me and your mother being together? As a couple? As your parents?

No. I remember Mom and Stan getting together. But that's it. Why? Are you trying to tell me something about you and your boyfriend? Are you in love with Jared, Dad?

She says it like she's teasing me.

I say, Yes, I am, but it's … serious but not marriage serious, and anyways, just because you're seeing someone doesn't mean you have to love someone.

She says, That's definitely true, then quickly says, I love you, and without waiting for me to say it back, she disconnects.

I hold the phone to my head for a second before putting it in my pocket and sauntering toward Nicks.

It's then that it hits me. My daughter doesn't remember the way her mother and I loved each other, doesn't remember the little things, like how we'd sit and eat dinner always next to each other, side by side, like how I'd kiss Betsy's shoulder when we greeted each other because of some joke when we first started hanging out about our being the same height. The way we linked arms instead of holding hands.

I walk past Mr. Delbert's old house. The chain link has been torn down, and a work crew has set posts to build a new wooden fence. The groove that ran along the inside of it when Mr. Dog paced back and forth is filled in with grass and weeds. Like the dog was never there.

The week Stella and I took care of Mr. Dog was the sweetest, most tender week we'd shared in a long time. It hurts me to think where Mr. Dog is now. Gone. The house too, with its new FOR SALE sign, because it sold not to a family but to a developer who's fixing it up and pricing it at twice what he bought it for. Like the neighborhood. Gone. Like everything goes. I'm feeling like hell.

Nicks is packed for a Tuesday, and I'm pissed about it. The owner thinks he's found his goldmine by cornering the market on karaoke. So suddenly every fucking night except Sundays karaoke begins about 9:30, or whenever Adam the Karaoke DJ gets there. I am frustrated. My routine is set. It works. I don't want to change it to Sunday or to another bar farther away.

A curve in the bar allows the few regulars to congregate a bit away from the younger crowd that shows up to sing and binge drink and heckle their friends. There I join Jason, who is also in some kind of mood. He's a bit quieter than usual. So we both just sip on our drinks, his a locally brewed IPA. I'm starting with sparkly water and a lime, figuring I should pace myself. We squint to watch Warriors highlights with the sound off as someone sings a rather good rendition of a Fleetwood Mac song. The carpet in the bar has been cleaned recently, so the place smells like flowery detergent and old onions.

Susan from Upstairs, who's ecstatic that karaoke is taking over the bar and dresses up like people are paying to hear her sing, wiggles in next to us as the crowd is trickling in. The lighting is low, and they've added laser lights along with a spotlight illuminating the Karaoke Korner, as it's now called. The words are stenciled in white on the blue walls behind the mic stand dancing with green and red patterned lights that keep time with the music.

I say, I hate that it's getting so crowded.

Susan says, I'm just tickled this old boring place has some life in it. She adjusts this large sequined handbag like she's proved her point.

I say, But now we can't even talk to each other or watch the basketball game. I motion to the TV.

Nobody can watch anything on that tiny old TV. And who likes basketball? she asks.

Jason says, I do.

And so do I, I say.

Bob says from a few feet away, I do too.

Well, the owner of the bar told me he likes money, and doesn't that end the conversation, Susan says and laughs.

Bob shakes his head and says, Yes, that does, and I do like tips.

Here's a tip, I say. How about respect your elders, and how about you fill up my sparkly water.

I smile at him, and he smiles back.

Are you an elder now? Susan asks.

I have a daughter about to be in college, I say.

When you have a granddaughter about to be in college, then you're an elder, Susan says and picks up her glass of red wine.

Something about Susan makes me soften. Mr. Delbert is gone, the neighborhood is a mess, my daughter leaving. I feel like I can't see anything positive. But I see Susan. Right in front of me. Dressed in fine attire and loving the singers so earnestly singing.

I ask, How many grandkids you got?

Three. One's twelve and the other two are twins, and they're four.

Twins. That's crazy parenting, I say, wondering what it would have been like to have had two Stellas.

Susan chuckles, shaking her head, and says, It certainly is, but I have no problems with that kind of crazy.

Her confidence invigorates me. She sits up higher on her stool and brags, In fact, I watch little Jordan and Jules Tuesdays and Thursdays. What else do I have to do but stress about that racist president or sit around and wait to sing?

That's brave, I say.

No, that's family.

Over the mic, Adam the Karaoke DJ announces, Susan! You're up next. Lovely Susan, where are you?

Watch this for me, will you sweetie, while I sing this song. Be careful with my purse. Don't spill anything on it, Susan says and pats my shoulder and struts up to the front of the bar like she's won some award.

I pull the bedazzled and glittering purse close to me.

Two guys, both with scruffy beards and puffy jackets, walk up and block our view of Susan singing some R&B from the '70s. I lean to the side to see. She's actually good, and people are, in fact, watching her.

One of the guys turns toward her for a minute, then leans back and says, That fat lady can sing.

And the other guy says, I hope the night ain't over yet.

They both start laughing and shout to Bob their order. Bob walks away to the beer cooler. I turn to Jason.

Did you hear that, I say.

What? He asks.

Those two guys called Susan fat.

Those two. Jason points.

Yes, I say, and realize I made a mistake. Jason doesn't fuck around, though I like that about him. His pock-marked face glows in the low light, both angelic and terrifying.

Hey, he calls out. Hey you.

One of the guys says, What's up, my man?

Don't call me my man when you just body-shamed my friend who's singing.

The guy with the beard turns to the other guy with the beard, and they both look to the Karaoke Korner and then to Bob, who is just smiling like he is waiting to see what might happen next.

The first guy with the beard says, Sorry, man. No disrespect.

Don't tell me that. You better tell her, Jason says.

Ok, he says and leaves a ten-dollar bill for two tall boys of PBR, which would have been only five dollars total, and walks to the front of the bar, as far from us as possible. Bob leans over and says, Do that shit more often.

What, stand up for someone? Jason asks.

Bob says, If it makes people tip a hundred percent, yes, please.

Jason says, Any time.

He salutes me with his glass, and I salute him back.

Sometimes you have to stand up for things even if it isn't about you, Jason says. He says it like a mantra. Like it's gospel.

Very true, I say. I don't get high, but I support legalizing weed.

40

No one calls it weed, Bob says. Clearly, you really don't get high.

I ignore him and say, Or you don't have to be gay to support same-sex marriage.

But you're gay, Bob says, aren't you?

He says this while washing glasses, casually, like he's commenting on the weather. I open my mouth. I close my mouth.

The moment you see yourself the way other people see you is traumatic. I have never taken Jared here. I have never talked about my lovers. I thought all Bob knew about me was that I have a daughter and an ex-wife. I feel hot. I feel Jason looking at me. I hear the music stop, and even though I know it's just a transition from one song to the next, the silence seems pregnant. I hear Susan walk up. I hear shouts from the bearded guys as a person they know takes the mic, and then the first chords to some Violent Femmes song.

I say, I'm queer. There's a difference. But that's not my point.

What's your point, Bob asks, still cleaning glasses, not looking at me.

My point is that . . . it's that we need . . . we all need each other at times.

Bob dries his hands on a dishtowel, nodding. He makes a serious face, his lips pursing together.

He says, That's nice, Juan. Really nice.

I can't tell if he means it or not. I can't tell if he's playing.

Susan says, Thanks for watching my bag. Bob, baby, can I get a glass of water please?

Certainly, Susan, he says and walks to grab it.

I add, And it's time for my Bulleit!

He waves to show that he heard me.

Jason pats my shoulder this time.

He says, One of these fucking nights, we should go up there and sing a song.

One of these nights, I say.

I spend the rest of the evening resisting the urge to sip malty bourbon after malty bourbon in order to suppress a gnawing desire for something I cannot name.

The next morning I bike to Jared's apartment along King Street. Thinking of him makes me smile. I recall how Jared informed me on our first date that I was a freak for never wearing ear buds, like apparently everyone else in the world, as I biked. I explained that I liked to pay attention to the world around me, to peep into the houses and hear people talking on the sidewalk.

That's some creepy male shit right there, he teased.

We met on Tinder. After texting one afternoon and the following morning, we agreed to just chill and go on a leisurely bike ride to the farmers market. He rode up on a cruiser with a removable metal shopping basket. His handlebars even had a bell. In the basket, a perfectly folded jacket. He wore new denim jeans and a t-shirt of the warmest blue. I wore khaki pants and a button-up flannel, red and black, basically the same outfit I had been wearing since I was twenty. I also had my fancy Bianchi Vigorelli, which felt a little garish compared to his.

After we locked them at the market, he stepped up to me, and I stood still, not sure what to do. He asked to hug me. I said yes. He smelled like exercise and mint. We entered Sweet Adeline Bakeshop and shared a donut muffin. He had a tea, and I had a macchiato. We bantered easily about the changing Bay Area, his distressing but obsessive love of hipster music, as he called it, like Elliott Smith and Bon Iver. I talked about my daughter. Then we strolled through the farmers market. He placed his produce in the basket and covered it with his folded jacket.

When we got on our bikes to ride away, I faced north on King and he faced south.

I live in Oakland, he said.

I live in Berkeley.

He said, I won't hold it against you. In fact, you can still kiss me goodbye if you want.

I want, I said, and leaned over to him, worried my breath smelled of stale coffee, but he didn't seem to mind.

It was a perfect first date.

The memory of his mouth makes me bike a little faster to get to his apartment this morning.

Though it's a workday, Jared has a medical appointment in the afternoon, so he's off from his job at the Green Brown Institute, an Oakland advocacy group working with people of color in the environmental industry.

I once teased him that mixing greens and browns made mud. He didn't think it was funny. He loves his job—explained with a straight back and hand gestures that it's one of the most effective ways to directly confront institutional and structural racism. Young people of color need to see themselves in the struggle to defend the environment because it's their heritage. Not just urban streets or sports fields, he lectured.

It both excited and scared me when he got going on his job or politics, because he had this way of sounding engaged and optimistic, unlike so many people who make everything so fucking dire. But I also worried that my job appeared self-indulgent.

He asked, Does your work make you happy?

I shrugged.

He said, Listen. My mother. She's a sweetheart. Trust me. But she was brutally honest. The best advice she gave me was that there is so much drama in the world, that as a black person—and of course you can extrapolate—but you have to hold tight to your joy. Make it your job. Your car or neighborhood. Make it your wife. It doesn't matter. They take so much away, don't let them take joy.

She said wife? I asked.

She was old school. But not dumb. He smiled at me with his perfect rectangular teeth and full lips.

And here he is giving me that same inviting smile as I sit on the bench seat in his breakfast nook while he makes our coffee.

Jared loves the word *nook*. When he was looking for an apartment, he filtered his search for the word, he told me. Like he was revealing something about himself. Something important.

I'm not even sure I know what *nook* means, I said.

Sure you do. It's a little space, a space you got to squeeze into, he said and squeezed the fingers on one hand into a little point.

Jared finishes the coffee and proceeds to slide close to me, taking up all of my personal space. He hands me a mug. I think of my conversation with Stella about marriage. Jared and I being a couple. A thing. In love. I have this momentary defensive reaction: It's not my fault. I didn't plan this. It happened by degrees.

But I did help facilitate it: the date night when we both logged on and updated our profiles to *in a relationship with*. The way he said in a deep voice how we were now Facebook official. I remember the confident and comfortable way we fucked that night. I like thinking of sex. Jared and I have playful sex that involves a lot of cuddling and cooing that makes me feel both adored and safe.

Lately, we've been consistent in our scheduling, which I think is synonymous with commitment, another marker of being a couple.

Still, he doesn't push too much, and I don't balk too much. So things just go along without too much drama. But I feel like he's waiting for something more.

Why do you love me? I ask Jared.

That's an unfair question, he says.

In what way? I ask.

Every way. It's not something I need to justify or explain. It just is.

He nudges me as he says this. I feel loved right then. It's his gift. To make people feel prioritized.

But if you need reasons, he says, you have panache without the flamboyance. There's a strength and a sadness to you. You make me think of hugging. Not pat-on-the-back hugs. Of big bear hugs.

That's just because of my belly, I say.

Oh, and there's that. What a nice belly you have, and a nice prominent nose and brow. It's manly and dignified. And your hair ... who can resist a nice fresh fade?

He softly places his hand on the back of my head. In my ears I hear the scratch, scratch of hair against his palm.

He asks, Have you ever grown out your hair?

I say, When I was younger, but now I go every other Friday to the barbershop up the street.

Why? He asks.

I like it that way.

You look good, he says.

Thank you.

I take his hand. I hold it. I think of the things I do that show him I care for him. I wonder if I would marry him. I wonder if I would marry anyone again.

I say, Next week you should come with me to Nicks. Sadly, it's now always karaoke.

Oh, I love karaoke, but do you really want me to? That seems like Juan's last non-Jared space?

I think maybe he's right, but say, Yes, please come. Because I did want him to met Jason and all the others I've talked about. Even so, my body clenches just a bit.

I mean, you don't need to come every single time I go, I say.

Well, you're in luck, because though I do love karaoke, I certainly don't want to witness it every time I go out, he says. But Juan, the invite means a lot because I know how much you enjoy *drinking nights*.

He uses air quotes to mock those nights' importance, and I feel a rush of shame.

But he then says, Seriously, I know how many close friends you have there. I know you're making room for me.

Thank you, I say. And I mean it.

Jason is certainly my friend. But I think of Bob the Bartender and Rachel. Susan from Upstairs. Frankie and his suit. Would they consider me friends?

I'll behave, he adds.

I pat his shoulder.

But not if you touch me like that. He growls and pushes me farther into his nook.

I leave him a few hours later. All weekend I think about the essay Stella's supposed to be writing. I call her Sunday morning, even though I will see her that night.

Is everything all right? She answers.

Yes. I pause and then say, You know me and your mom. We loved each other but barely knew each other or ourselves back then. I'm glad I married her, though. I'd do it again.

Ok, she says like she's not following me.

I say, And I like marriage, and if I wanted to marry a man, it would be nice to have that option.

Ok, she says like she's thinking. I promise if you ever marry again, I'll be right there for you, Dad. I'll be your best daughter and give you away.

I smile.

I love you, Dad, she says.

I love you too.

I have to go, she says and hangs up without waiting for my response.

Tuesday night comes, and I meet Jared in front of Nicks. As I walk up I hear a Cake song through the walls. Jared's talking to a slightly disheveled young man sitting on a stool checking IDs. Tuesday nights never used to have a door person. I flush with irritation. This guy is small, but something about him feels tightly coiled. Like you do not want to piss him off. He's reading a cheap sci-fi paperback and explaining to Jared how most non-black people are shocked that he's reading sci-fi.

Jared says, You should act all confused. Like you had no idea you were reading a book.

The guy says, What! This is a book, not a blunt?

They laugh, and I laugh a bit too loudly, and they both look at me.

Jared says to the guy, Nice talking to you, and now I'm going to go buy my boyfriend a drink.

My body stiffens as Jared takes my hand.

The other man watches this and says, That's cool, but I'm still gonna need to see your ID.

We post up in the corner of the bar. Everyone is there. Susan from Upstairs and Jason and Frankie wearing the same chocolate-brown suit. Bob the Bartender, of course, and his girlfriend Rachel as well.

My throat tightens and my armpits sweat. I feel exposed. But I'm determined. I wave Bob over.

Bob. This is Jared. Bob is the bartender, I say.

Obviously, Jared says.

Bob places both hands under his chin like he's posing and then glides them across the bartop.

But, I add, struggling to make eye contact with Bob, he's also a writer and a damn good karaoke singer.

Thank you, Juan, for noticing.

Nice to finally meet you, Jared says.

Jason, before I get a chance to say anything, simply hugs Jared.

I do the rounds: Susan and Frankie and Rachel and anyone else I have met before.

I make introductions. I welcome him in.

Jared is affable and relaxed and wins them all over.

There are also a lot of young folks with cans of beer and shots of cheaper whiskey than I drink. We ignore them mostly until Susan makes her move to sing. She gives me her purse again.

Jared tells her he loves it. He says, It's just like my mother's.

Susan leans over to me and says, I like him.

I look at Jared like I've never seen him before. Susan belts out a rendition of a Tina Turner song. We all hoot and howl as it ends. I see some cute group of friends get up next and do some Neil Diamond song about turning on your heart light.

They're pretty good, Jared says.

Jason says, You know what? It's time we got our asses up there.

Bob says, If you guys want to go up there, I'll join you, and I can get us up there any time we want. Because I'm the bartender. He smiles triumphantly.

If the bartender offers to sing, there is a universal rule that you must take him up on it, Jason says.

I think there is a law in a few states about that, Jared says.

I kick his foot. He laughs.

Jason says, I have the perfect song. He flips through the red binder of pages. The binder irritates me because who ever put it together alphabetized *the* in the song titles.

Jason says, I guarantee we all know this song.

He shows Bob and me, and Bob smiles and says, Let's do this.

Of course I know it, I say.

I try to show Jared, but he says, Oh no. I want the surprise.

I grab his hand to make him come up there with me, but he slips it out of my grasp.

Jason takes off his jacket, but he doesn't stop there. He takes off his black t-shirt with the logo of some punk band. He's in only a white tank top, and I can smell him, biting but manly.

I haven't had my Bulleit yet but, there's no time. Bob is walking to the front of the bar. The crowd goes wild because the bartender is up there. He waves Jason and me up, and we all crowd around one mic. The familiar epic beginning to "Sweet Child o' Mine" starts. Jason grabs the mic stand and does the Axel Rose dance. People start to clap and cheer. We all start singing, and I look out into the audience. Susan covers her ears. I see her laugh though and smile. I see Jared doing the same thing. Laughing and smiling. Twenty or so unknown patrons laughing and smiling.

And singing. Everyone's singing.

It makes me sing louder.

It makes Jason dance more.

It makes Bob jump up and down.

I sing my heart out. I close my eyes and belt out lyrics like I truly mean them, like it doesn't matter who's watching me or what they see.

5

Sandy Balls and Smiles

If you ask me, and I know you didn't, but just hear me out, Jason says.

I shake my head, knowing this conversation is going nowhere fast. But I can't help it. I smile and turn to him on the bar stool and wait.

Jason says, If you've never worn a speedo in public on a beach, then that just says something about you. Jason states this loudly. Like a proclamation. Like a dare.

I'm sharing with him the dilemma I face. I'm about to meet Jared's closest friends, Patti and Damian, at his work party on Stinson Beach. When Jared asked me to accompany him, I cautioned that we'd never been swimming together before.

He said, There are lots of things we haven't done yet together. Long road trips in a car. Skydiving. Family gatherings. Why are you so concerned by swimming?

Jared held my hand as we strolled through the neighborhood along King Street—a pre-dinner constitutional, a new habit we were trying to form—the sun streaking the sky, neighbors out front or on little stoops. I pulled him quickly past Mr. Delbert's old home, where a new family was moving in, all smiles and excitement.

Speaking of family gatherings, Stella's graduation is in a couple weeks at the Greek Theater, I said.

Yikes, are you ready? I know all about graduation at the Greek. I had three cousins graduate from Berkeley High, and my mom forced me to go to each one.

You sound angry.

Just you wait. Hours of torture. But it's fun to see how the families go all wild.

I wondered if I'd go wild as Jared said, but I don't think so because I'm not sure how I feel about her graduating. It means her leaving.

So. You want to come with me? I asked.

You're coming with me to my work party at Stinson, right?

I squeezed his hand and said, Deal. Somehow that feels fair. Though I should make you help shop for her graduation dresses too.

Relationships are never quite fair, Jared said. And what do you mean *dresses*?

One for graduation. One for the graduation party.

Of course. He laughed. But answer my question about swimming. Why does that make you nervous?

I don't quite know, I said. I used to swim all the time with Stella and her friends. We'd go to Willard Pool, and when they got older I'd take them to the Yuba River. Now I'm not sure I still own a pair of swim shorts.

Jared said, I don't own a pair of swim shorts.

Then how are you going to swim?

I only wear speedos.

I didn't know what to say to that, though I did immediately imagine him in a speedo.

You fucking with me? I asked.

Jared said, I'd never fuck with you. Devilish grin on his face, his body sporting this form-fitting super-soft sweater. I could feel the cuffs of it tickling my wrist.

He said, I don't care what you wear. You just have to come. I want to show you off to my friends, who are beginning to believe you don't really exist.

That's why I made the bad decision of asking Jason where to get swim shorts in Oakland, also relaying Jared's swimsuit preference.

I say, Jason, I know you like to think everything is political, but that's just plain stupid.

And not true, Frankie says.

We're posted up at Nicks. The crowd's light tonight, but it's still an hour before karaoke begins, so we are able to talk and stare at sports highlights on the TV. Jason can't contradict Frankie. Jason may be able to shit talk and provoke random strangers and even close friends, but he won't argue with an elder.

Frankie sips his gin and tonic through his little black straw and waits, refusing to elaborate.

Fine, Jason says. But it's got some truth to it.

Frankie says flatly, Just because it's true doesn't make it correct. Most of Europe wears speedos. At least they did when I was stationed over there. But in the US nobody does, though I'd agree with you that most haven't tried speedos either.

I tried, Jason brags.

Bob walks over. Tried what?

Don't ask, I say.

Speedos, Jason explains. But I didn't like them. So now I don't wear anything. Free-balling in the Bay.

We all groan.

Bob asks like he's really curious, Where are there nude beaches?

Jason says, There's Baker Beach that's clothing optional. There's Muir Beach. The far end of Stinson Beach. He pats me on the back. Maybe you won't even need a pair of shorts.

I say, Maybe I don't.

Man, only three official naked beaches? Bob says as he wipes the counter.

The US is so fucking uptight, Jason says.

Or perhaps we just don't want to see your ball sack, Frankie says.

We all freeze because Frankie in fancy attire just said *ball sack*.

I can't help but tease Jason. I love ball sacks, but I'd probably be ok with not seeing random and various ones covered in sand.

Sandy balls are the worst, Jason agrees.

Indeed, Frankie adds.

We all laugh, but Frankie doesn't flinch. Just raises his glass again and sips.

Frankie, I ask, when were you in Europe?

From '74 through '76. I traveled all over Europe with the Army Corps of Engineers.

Really?

And Africa in '77.

Damn.

And Brazil '78 through '80.

Jason and I look at each other.

Frankie breathes in deeply and says, People need travel to be able to imagine other ways of doing something. I raised my kids on army bases around the world. Saw people doing all kinds of things we don't do here in the States. Definitely not here in Oakland. Some I tried and loved, like surfing and vegemite, and some I tried and hated, like speedos, and I learned that most things people do really make no sense unless you been doing it all your life. Happy to know my kids understand that.

How many do you have? I asked, realizing with some shame that I was about to learn something I should have already known.

Two.

How often do you see them? I asked.

Not enough. He raises his drink and sips. I wonder if he is disappointed. Lonely.

Wait, can we get back to surfing? Jason asks.

Loved it. Went to South Africa to surf J-Bay.

All the way to Africa? Why? California has all the surfing you could want.

He says, I was in Africa when the opportunity presented itself. But to be honest, I was thankful it happened there. I didn't really want to see a bunch a white hippie kids surfing. It was the late '70s. I wanted to see some black folks surfing.

And what was that like? Jason asks.

Wouldn't know. Not that many black folks were surfing. White people are everywhere. Frankie chuckles at his own comment, like that might have been the funniest, truest thing anybody's ever concluded.

Do you miss your kids? I ask.

I do, but they're out there doing their thing. Traveling. Working. Couldn't be more proud.

Frankie, Jason says all serious like. Let me ask you something. You've been coming here long enough that maybe you know. Why did Nick leave out the apostrophe in the sign?

The sign's not missing an apostrophe, because it's not a name. It's a greeting. Back in the day you used to ask a friend how he was doing, and he'd say *nicking and grinding*, which got shortened to something like *nicks, man, nicks*. And so Nicks was born.

Jason and I stare at Frankie.

Did you know this, Bob? I ask.

I don't even think the owner knows this.

Jason says, Wow. I know the Bay Area has a rich history of linguistic playfulness.

Like hella and hyphy, he says.

Don't say that again, I threaten.

Or hammer time, Bob yells from a few feet away. And does an MC Hammer dance. He's surprisingly good at it.

Jason says, You know what's shitty, Frankie? You have all these stories, but the only place I can imagine you in is this bar in that fancy suit.

That, my friend, says something about you more than you wearing a speedo or going rogue, as we called skinny dipping in the army, Frankie says.

It's a lack of imagination, I tease and push Jason.

Or it's an example of my internalized racist mindset, Jason says in such a somber tone I feel the need to soothe him. But I don't. Because I know what he means. I think of the people in my life and how limited my knowledge of them is. How I miss out on who they are by holding on to only what I empirically know: Bob behind his bar. Jason riding his barstool like a high horse. Stella on her phone. Jared in his nook.

I wait until the day before we've planned to drive up to Stinson Beach to buy my suit. I've never been a big shopper—usually walk in, grab what I want, and walk out.

It's Saturday, and Stella is in her room. I knock. She's cleaning it. She has her earbuds in and doesn't notice me. I stand and watch her for that second before she realizes I'm there, and something about the scene is beautiful.

What the hell, Dad. Knock!

I did.

I didn't hear you.

Hence me opening the door.

No, hence you waiting and knocking harder.

She's right, I know. But I don't back down. I don't say sorry. I stare at her. She stares back. But I don't want to fight. I see her stacks of folded clothes and boxes of papers and stuff. I'm feeling both nostalgic and emotional. All bunched up.

I ask, Do you want to go shopping for your graduation dresses today?

Maybe. She relaxes a bit.

Plus, I need to get a bathing suit.

As soon as I say this, I realize it's a little strange. Or is it? I'm confused. Would it be inappropriate to shop for a bathing suit with my daughter? It's a question of boundaries and relationships. I don't bring up that I'm considering speedos.

I ask, How long has it been since we've been swimming? I can't even find my old pair of shorts.

That ratty old orange pair you always wore. That's probably a good thing. Let me finish here, and we can go to Bay Street, she says and breathes in and looks around her room. Determined and focused.

Do you want some coffee? I ask, not quite wanting to leave her yet.

She looks directly at me and says, Yes, please. And then she smiles. And it's so intense that in her smile I can see her as a newborn, as a laughing child, as a ridiculous teenager, and now as a young adult. Smiles never change.

I prepare the coffee to perfection. Holding the kettle with one hand, I pour at a nice even pace into the Melitta as I stir with the other hand.

We both drink it black. It felt like victory when she finally acquiesced to the way I make coffee and not her mother: creamy and sweet.

I stand at her door, now shut again, holding both cups. I say, Stella.

Nothing. I have no other option. I bang on the door with my forehead and smile at my own stupidity as coffee sloshes over the rim of each mug.

She opens it and says, Remember this? and holds up a stuffed sloth.

It's Ugly Perezosa, I say loudly.

From Abuela, she says.

At her feet there's a small box bursting open with stuffed animals: frogs, a turtle, a toucan. And of course a plastic crucifix and a rosary.

One thing my mother loves besides Jesus is jungle animals, and she gave Stella one every Christmas.

I set down the mugs and sit on the floor next to her and the box. We try to remember all the names she gave each one.

What'd you call the frog?

Leggy.

That's right. And the turtle?

Old Man.

And the toucan?

PicaPica.

You saved them all, I marvel.

Of course, I did. I called Abuela a few days ago and told her how much I appreciated her gifts. Why don't you see her more often?

I say, She might give you stuffed animals. She gives me nothing but shit.

Dad, Stella says. That's such a lie. You never visit her. You never give her a chance.

Mothers and grandmothers are such different things.

Are you going to be any different?

When you have a child? I ask like I'm shocked and scared of the possibility.

Yes. I'll have kids one day.

I'll probably be a lot meaner, since with you I was so damn nice.

Right, she says.

Why'd you call her?

I call her a lot. Like once a month. More than you, she tells me. I call her.

Did you invite her to graduation?

I hadn't, and I have this *oh fuck* moment. I want to text Betsy and ask if she invited her own parents.

Stella throws Ugly Perezosa at me and says, No wonder you don't get stuffed animals.

You invited her?

57

I did.

Did you invite your mother's parents?

I invited them but knew they probably wouldn't come from Tucson. They did offer to send money to help with my move and stuff.

I'm proud of you, Stella.

Thanks. She nods. I know you are. Then she says, And since you are so proud of me and all the hard work I'm doing, perhaps you can buy me just one dress and use the rest of the money to get me a car. That way I could also drive to see Abuela when I'm back in town.

I'm not that proud of you, I say and throw Ugly Perezosa back at her.

She drives us to the Bay Street mall in my Mercedes and talks nonstop about school and hunting for an apartment on Facebook and how she really really really needs a car in LA. I just smile and listen and ask questions. I try really really really hard not to offer advice or make suggestions or any other kind of parental guidance.

In H&M, the attendant informs Stella that she can only bring seven items into the stall, so Stella makes me wait right outside holding her extra three dresses as she bounces away into the changing room. The attendant smiles and she slides me a chair.

Each dress Stella tries on is skimpier and more risqué than the previous—one that almost entirely exposes her back in a swooping V, one in gold lamé that's skin tight with slits that reach to the tops of her thighs. As she changes, she lectures me about my mother, then steps out and spins in front of the mirror.

You and Abuela aren't so different.

I'm not like my mother. At all.

She studies me. This dress is white, lined with frills that bounce along the hemline and across the chest with every movement. A go-go-girl style. She says, You're not really, but you act the same about certain things.

What things?

Emotions, she whirls. But I understand, she continues as she steps back into the changing room.

You understand what? I yell after her, and the attendant looks at me.

I can't imagine the family drama with your father, she yells back.

You didn't try to invite him, did you? Clearly he can't come, I say. I want it to sound like I'm joking, because we both know he's been in jail for the last eighteen years. But it doesn't sound funny.

See, that's exactly what I mean, she shouts.

I get up and edge closer to the dressing rooms, reluctant to appear a weird older guy in the women's changing area, but right then she steps out dressed in her normal cut-off denims and BHS soccer shirt.

I want this one. She holds up the gold lamé gown.

What about these? I say, lifting the dresses I'm still holding, hoping there's one in the bunch with a bit more fabric.

Nah. Let's go get your swim shorts.

I quickly place the dresses in a ball on the attendant's counter trying not to make eye contact and rush after my daughter.

Finish what you were saying, I say as I catch up. She is casually flipping through racks on the way to the front door.

You guys seem awkward when it comes to expressing feelings. Like you're scared or nervous.

I express emotions.

Dad, you're like the most uncomfortable-looking guy in the world when Jared is affectionate to you around me.

I am not.

Just like Abuela. Not about romantic feelings, obviously, but when I say I miss her or when I ask how she's doing. Like really doing. It's so hard for her to say anything other than *I'm fine*.

Not every conversation needs to be so intimate. Not everyone needs to know everything about you, I say.

That's a slippery slope.

But that's the truth.

Only if you want it to be, Dad. She walks out the door and into a friend who's also shopping with her mother. The friend loves the dress. I make eye contact with the mother, and we half smile at each other.

Dad, can I go with Juliana to help her get her dress? And then she'll drive me home.

I want to say something about my bathing suit, but instead I respond, Sure, that's no problem.

Dad, Stella says. That's what I'm talking about. Are you sure?

It's fine. Go.

Just get a nice pair of surf shorts. Nothing too tight or small, she instructs.

What about a speedo?

You're joking, right?

I shrug. She gives me the evil eye, and I watch her move through the racks of clothes, loudly talking with her friend.

The mother steps up and sighs and says, Only a few months more before they're gone, but to be honest, I can't wait. Right? She smiles at me.

I nod, but after a second I say, It makes me sad.

She reaches out to place her hand on my shoulder, looking like she's trying to find something to say, but then just lets her hand drop and walks after them.

I find the one sports store in the mall, head right to the bathing-suit section, and grab a big pair of generic blue-and-white striped surfing shorts that hang to my knee. After a pause I grab a large black-and-orange speedo too. For a moment I consider trying them on. I shake my head and walk right up to the cashier with both suits in my hands.

6

The Greatest Moment on Earth

We are in Jared's place all packed up and ready to spend the day at Stinson Beach. Jared makes the eggs. I do the coffee. These are our roles. Relationships are not shaped by gender or destiny or love but by personal predilections: diet, bedtimes, alcohol consumption. Totally random and pointless things. Things you cannot predict. For example, if one person likes to stay up late while the other person goes to bed early, eventually the relationship will snap. All the talk of complementary patterns or the idea of balancing each other out is nice but not true. And if it ever does work out, it's an anomaly.

I make the coffee because I have a thing with coffee. He will drink anything that's brown. He doesn't mind burnt diner coffee, cold day-old coffee, even instant coffee.

In some ways, he's more adept at surviving in the world than I am. Meaning he is generally a happier, more satisfied person on a daily basis. He's learned to be open, learned to accept, learned tolerance, learned to be with the world not against it. I know it's just coffee, but still.

I remember when I explained to Jared that I'd make the coffee.

The only person I'll let make me a cup of coffee is my mama, I said.

You might need to unpack all the weird shit behind that statement, Jared said.

That did come out a bit weirder than I wanted it to. But the point is still valid. Out of respect for our relationship, out of wanting to be in a relationship, I really should make the coffee.

That's fine with me, Jared said. I love coffee made for me. Will you bring it to me as well? In bed? Please.

I gave him a look to signify this was not something to joke about.

Fine, Jared said, but will you at least bring it to me in my nook?

I'd be happy to.

Jared asked, Do you have a thing with eggs? How about I make the eggs? He says this like he's joking, like only a complete freak would have a thing about coffee *and* about eggs.

I said, No. I don't have a thing with eggs, shaking my head as if the question is ridiculous.

Then I said, Yes, actually, yes. I do have a thing with eggs. I can't eat them, can't even look at them, if they are runny. Ever since Stella and I killed one of the chickens we used to have, it's just really difficult for me to eat any chicken-related thing.

Now, as we're preparing to leave for Stinson, Jared says, Will you please, please tell me the story about killing the chicken with Stella?

I take a sip from my cup, and the coffee is perfect. It makes me relax. I slide into Jared's nook.

I say, We had four chicks. Three were hens, but one turned out to be a rooster. And it was mean. We tried to keep it, but it would just torment the other chickens. Pull feathers out. They were damn near plucked. But what was worse, this rooster would bite their cute red combs. I had no idea how much those things could bleed. I was trying to be all self-sufficient, raising chickens and telling myself I could kill and eat them if I needed to. Lo and behold, I had this rooster I couldn't get rid of, so here's a chance to teach my daughter something about responsibility.

I laugh at my ridiculousness, and Jared laughs with me. His eyes are bright in the morning sun coming through the windows. He looks beautiful standing in his kitchen, with sweat pants on and no shirt, cooking eggs. I see the band of his tighty non-whitey underwear, as he likes to call them. His face is stubbly and shadowed.

I say, My daughter was horrified. She was like eleven and thought those damn chickens were part of the family. Betsy had just moved out. It was an ugly time. And that rooster was hurting the others. Stella said she could handle it when I told her what we needed to do. We thought about and prepared for it. I didn't want to do it in the yard because the space was communal, so we decided to do it in the kitchen. We got the rooster to the sink, and after we calmed it down, I made my daughter hold the neck out long.

Jared says, How'd you calm it down?

I say, We sang to it. It made these soft sounds. Like it was joining in with our singing. Like it was happy.

Jared puts down the spatula and says, You seriously are telling me you both sang to the chicken to calm it down, and then you chopped its head off?

Exactly. Well, I tried to cut its head off, but it was my first time, and I didn't quite know which kind of knife to use. I grabbed this serrated one. I had to saw it like four or five times. The neckbone is a hard thing to break. Once the head came off, I tossed the body in the sink, but the chicken kept bouncing around. Stella was freaking out. She wanted to hold it, to stop the poor thing from jumping around, so I picked it up again and she helped me hold it tight. She told me she could feel its heart beating really fast, and then the heart just stopped. My daughter started crying. I started crying. We just held each other with this dead bleeding chicken between us.

I stop telling the story and sip my coffee. I nod to his cup, sitting across from me.

He says, You do know that's a fucked-up story. What did you do with it?

I say, We ate it. But it was a somber event. I haven't really eaten chicken since.

He brings the eggs on two plates. They're scrambled hard, with some sharp cheese in them and green onions.

Here you go, he says. You don't have to feel bad about these eggs. These were made with love by cage-free chickens that flutter about northern California.

Happy eggs, I say and smile.

Happy eggs, he repeats as he scooches into his breakfast nook.

We tap the rims our coffee mugs, and Jared laughs.

What? I say.

I'm just thinking what my mother would say if she heard that story.

What would she say?

She'd say, *Is that boy crazy?*

He made his voice faster and pitched it higher.

I ask, Does your mother know how you imitate her?

My mama didn't raise a fool. I would never let her hear me do that.

What did she raise?

A critical thinking skeptical motherfucker.

Really? And how'd she do that?

Jared thinks for a few seconds. I have never met his mother, but he's described her as tall, thin, sweet, and angry.

Jared says, She told me believe half of what people say and all of what they do.

Sounds like my dad.

But unlike your dad, she also told me to be myself and let other people be themselves.

Sounds like good advice.

She may not have been the most empathetic person, but she certainly was wise.

Jared may be loving and kind in his nook, but traffic brings out the evil in him. Winding down Panoramic Highway, his usually calm and roll-with-it demeanor turned dour. We barely said a word the last hour, which was fine because I felt anxious.

Now we stand on Stinson Beach about a hundred yards from the shore. The sun glares. A light wind blows. The sand burns as we hurry, me gripping my beach bag that holds my two pairs of shorts and towel, Jared carrying two bottles of rosé we picked up from Trader Joe's, to the area set up with tents and tables and beach chairs. The scene is right out of some hip, feel-good car commercial—a diverse slice of Bay Area life with people mingling around in mini circles, laughing, holding beer cans in cozies, soft hip-hop playing out of someone's portable device. A group kicks a soccer ball. A table offers food, each dish labeled clearly with signs: gluten free, vegetarian, or vegan. And donuts.

I wrap myself in a towel, an old one of Stella's covered in tropical fish, and say to Jared quietly, Wait a second. Everybody's wearing normal shorts.

Jared stares at me like he has no idea what I'm talking about.

The speedos. You said you only wore speedos.

Oh no. Are you serious? Jared whispers, wrapping his much more adult red beach towel around his waist to change into his regular-looking swim shorts. He continues, I thought you knew I was joking. You didn't really get a speedo, did you?

I breathe and consider lying, but I want to be more open with my emotions. I say, I didn't want to embarrass you, so yes, I bought a pair of each kind of suit. Just in case.

He cocks his head, his look pure delight, and hugs me.

He whispers, If you want to put them on for me tonight, I'd be happy to take them off.

I push him off me and look around.

These are all the people you work with? Everyone's so young and . . . and cool.

You chose yourself a winner, Jared says and unwraps his towel to reveal his sexy thighs, muscled and appearing perpetually flexed.

He has donned light-blue swim shorts, tight and falling only half-way down his thighs.

My striped shorts hang way past my knee, and the waist is too loose. I'm both appalled and delighted. Maybe all that biking has helped. Maybe I've lost weight. But now my very pale ass is hanging out of the top of my shorts because they won't stay on. I look at the tag: XL.

Ugh.

Jared laughs and whispers, Maybe you should put on them speedos, after all.

Up stroll Jared's friends Patti and Damian. I face them holding up my shorts. Jared puts his arm around me and says, This is my partner, Juan.

Patti, holding a Frisbee, says, It's about time we met you. He keeps you so well hidden.

We talk and toss the Frisbee, surprisingly easy to do while using one hand to hold up my shorts. We eat and drink, and everyone is so pleasant.

The four of us lounge on our towels, sunscreened and glistening in the sunshine. They tried to make some agreement about not talking about work, but since I'm new and nervous and trying to pay attention, I ask questions about their jobs.

You really take ninety middle-school kids on overnight field trips? I ask Patti.

Damian says, She takes them to Tahoe to measure the snowcap. She's Colombian and obsessed with anything related to winter. Makes no sense.

It's true, says Patti. I even lead snowboarding camp.

What happened in your childhood? Jared asks.

Patti doesn't flinch. Honestly, my childhood sucked. I didn't even like to read, but I spent hella time in the library just to be anywhere but my house.

Looking at picture books? Damian asks.

Hella picture books. I loved the ones about geology and science. And most were in English, so whatever, I couldn't even read them if I wanted to. But the pictures of snow. The ones about climate and the world's environment. That's all I wanted. To get away from where I was. She continues, Guess that's one good thing about the fucked-up US policies. They led to my family fleeing here.

Illegally, right? Damian asks, and I can't tell if he's serious or fucking with her.

Of course. Tell me when the US ever welcomed refugees, Patti jokes.

They all laugh. For some reason, the way they tease and banter makes me tense. They're so relaxed, familiar with one another. Like family. I feel my body sweating in the sun, and then feel Jared's hand reaching for mine.

Patti looks at me and says, When I got here, my first semester in middle school, there was this teacher whose education philosophy was all about taking kids places. We did a trip in the fall to the César Chávez National Monument. The next semester, we went to the Tule internment camp.

Incarceration camp, Jared says. I look at him, because he sounds just like Jason, correcting someone over the politics of their word choice.

Right. Thank you, Patti responds. But the best thing for me was the snow all around the camp. So there you go.

She says, Now I lead children into nature.

Damian adds, Predominantly children of color, no less. From Oakland and Richmond and Vallejo. You do good work, my love. He pats her arm.

That's right, because this is our heritage, too, Patti says and rolls on her back, extending her arms skyward. She then does some young person's flip from her back to standing and races through a few scattered groups, yelling for people to join her. She sprints across the scorching sand to the water.

Damian laughs.

I ask Jared, How old is she?

Ah, to be that young again. Want to swim?

I do.

Jared looks at Damian and says, If I beat you, you gotta file all the progress reports next week.

Damian says nothing, but bounds up and takes off. Jared howls and races behind him. I watch their bodies bounce away, then stand and take off after them, feeling my belly and chest jiggle, the uncomfortable angle of my arm holding up my shorts, my other arm flapping wildly, my gait awkward from trying desperately not to touch longer than necessary on the burning sand. For a second, I wonder how I look, but as the water approaches, blue and calm and accepting, I simply don't care. I hit the water and feel my shorts slide right out of my hand and down my legs.

As I surface and scramble to pull up my suit, I hear Patti and Jared laughing, then Patti yells something about being blinded by the glare off my ass cheeks.

Damian points and says, There's a nudie beach just down the way, behind those rocks.

I smile and say, I actually already know that.

On the drive home, I break it to Jared that my mother will be accompanying us to the graduation ceremony.

Oh, damn, he says and raises his eyebrows. I see bits of sand stuck in his hair. He glows from the sun and excitement.

He says, Today was great. I feel great. Bring on your mama. I'm ready. He puts his arm around me as I drive, and I have this rush of apprehension.

Rarely do I think of my father locked away in Salinas Valley State Prison. I don't think about him for a lot of reasons. But he used to say, If it's pretty and it's free, don't trust it. In fact, he said that when

I first told him about Betsy and me. He said it whenever something good happened to me.

Jared. He feels too good. So much so that I don't trust it. Or myself.

I keep my distance over the next few days. I stay busy wrapping up a few client projects. It's pleasurable work because it's distracting work. I put more energy into it than I would normally, but sometimes you need to just put one foot in front of the other. Rein it in. Stay calm and focused.

If Jared notices my withdrawal, he doesn't say anything when I text that we should meet at the Greek Theater right before graduation begins. I don't invite him to the pre-graduation brunch. It's just too much.

At ten on the dot, my mother knocks on my door. She stands in the doorway in denim pants, light flannel shirt tucked in, and her old woven leather belt cinched at her waist. Her hair cut short, silver and black, her lips a deep red, the only makeup she wears. She looks surprisingly good. And happy.

She holds a gift bag with a wrapped present and a clearly visible stuffed owl wearing a graduation cap. With the other hand,

Good to see you, Mama, I say in the flattest tone possible. But when we hug I feel my body relax into it. Moms can always do that.

I love you, I say. Can you believe my little girl is graduating!

Can you believe she has the *cajones* to call and ask to buy my car? She has this whole plan to get her all set up in LA. She thrusts at me a single car key with a small metallic crucifix as the key ring. It's the spare, she says and steps in. You can pay the rest later.

What? You're selling her your car?

No. She pats my shoulder. I'm selling you and Betsy my old Nissan Sentra. You can mail a check. It's not like you to have cash on hand. You look good. A little heavier, but good.

She settles herself on my couch. I'm still holding the door open.

I say, Mom. Jared, my friend, wants to join us at the graduation?

The word *friend* comes so easily I shock myself, though I hate the questioning tone I hear in my voice, which puts the choice into my mom's hands. My jaw's clenched tight.

Juanito, have some respect. Don't you think this should be family only? Not some playtime with friends, she says.

The way she pronounces *friends* says it all. I remember Stella's remark about our not sharing emotions. How wrong she is. We can share everything in a single word.

I nod. I walk to my room and text Jared: Call me. Bad news.

He calls in less than a minute.

You all right? he asks.

Yes. But my mom brought a friend, so I need to use the ticket I had for you.

He says nothing.

Jared?

Juan, you know you can just buy a ticket at the Greek. It's not like it's sold out.

I didn't know this. I feel trapped and angry at everything around me. My mom. Myself. Jared.

Juan, it's ok. I get it. But you don't have to lie to me. That's the worst.

I'm sorry, I say, and there's a pause as he waits for more. It is my mom. She is just so . . . I can't finish the thought.

Jared says, Listen, I'd love to meet your mother. But to be honest, the last thing I want to do is sit in the blazing sun watching high-school students graduate. You're lucky. If this was a wedding with bad wedding dancing, you couldn't weasel your way out of inviting me.

Thank you, I say, both relieved and disturbed by how grateful I feel.

We'll talk later, he says ominously. Hey, but give Stella a hug for me and remember: bring seat cushions and water and sunscreen. Trust me.

I will.

When I step into the living room, my mother stands, holding her gift bag.

Have you heard from my father lately?

No. It's the same. I write. It gets returned. I save each one so if he ever says something about me not trying to stay in contact, I can slap down stacks of letters.

I don't even write anymore.

You know he doesn't want you to.

I quickly grab the bag that still has my beach towel and sunscreen in it. I throw in some water bottles. I point to the bag she's holding with the graduating stuffed owl poking out. You never gave me this many gifts, I say.

I didn't know you wanted stuffed animals, she responds.

Funny, I say and hold the door open for her.

I gave you your dad's watch.

I asked for it.

You get what you ask for.

She leans up and kisses me as she walks out.

At the graduation, Betsy and I are emotional and bored. My mother is just bored. Betsy's face is covered in these large aviator sunglasses and shaded by a floppy gardening hat. Even so, her face glows in afternoon sun. My mother sits next to her, holding the handles of her gift bag, tapping her feet like she's waiting to be called in a doctor's exam room.

I should have trusted Jared and stopped at Walgreens to purchase seat cushions, but I'm so glad I brought the water and sunscreen. When I reach for a bottle, I realize the speedo is still inside.

I offer sunscreen to Betsy. She's impressed that I'm so prepared.

We sit on the solid-rock benches. I spread the beach towel over the surface of the stone, and we sit directly facing the sun all afternoon as students give speeches, perform dance routines, hand out awards. The administration gives short peppy lectures about life and how to live it. All the while in the graduates' seating section—a wild mix of yellow and red—gowned students swat beach ball after beach ball as security runs after each one. The students try to keep them away. And each time the security team gets one of the balls, they pop it, eliciting a loud boo and hiss from the audience.

Then the roll call starts. There are names of kids we have watched grow up, who have been in and out of Stella's classes all her life. Betsy and I wax nostalgic about sleepovers and YMCA swim lessons and dance lessons and soccer fields.

Betsy begins to cry. Not a loud sobbing cry but a joyous quiet one. I don't even realize she's crying till she laughs and snuffles and hugs my mother.

Why are you crying? You never cry?

I cry all the time now.

Getting soft in your old lady age.

She slaps me on the shoulder. No, she says. But I don't hold back anymore. I'm not ashamed anymore.

You didn't even cry when we signed divorce papers. What were you ashamed of?

I was ashamed of failing. Of being a bad mom. Come on, Juan. I never wanted the divorce. That doesn't mean it wasn't necessary, she says, lowering her voice.

I think of asking why it was necessary. But I know why. It was necessary like change is necessary. Like kids leaving. Like mistrusting pretty things to protect yourself. Like writing letters despite their never being opened.

Plus, she says, look at our baby down there.

They're at the Gs, my mother says, reaching into her bag to hand us bottle poppers.

I can't help but laugh. She's not going to hear these, I say.

It's not for her. It's for us. To celebrate, she says, shaking her head.

Look how quickly everything goes, Betsy says.

I look down, and in the sea of red-and-yellow gowns, cheer after cheer goes up for each student. In the amphitheater seating, after each name is called, a mini-celebration happens, air horns wail, streamers get thrown, hoarse voices yell as loudly as possible names and declarations of love.

And then the announcer says it. Stella Gutiérrez.

The three of us go wild. We jump up, pop our bottle poppers, scream *Stella, we love you!* and embrace. Like it's the greatest moment on earth.

7

Big Familia

So you're telling me the first time you sucked a dick was with Betsy, the soon to be mother of your child? Jared asks.

When you say it like that, it sounds perverted, I say and fiddle with the elastic in my spandex shorts.

Absolutely not. When I say it like that, it sounds kind of hot. Jared leans in and bumps me.

We're standing on this little walking/biking bridge between Lake Merritt and Laney College. It's a late summer day, and the sky is a sharp blue. It's the morning of Stella's last day in the Bay. She's brunching with her friends now, but she informed me she'd like the pleasure of my company for a farewell dinner at Betsy's. Our partners are welcome to come.

This was conveyed in a new group text chain she named Big Familia. I smiled realizing Big Familia contained only three people. When I texted her this, Stella responded, It's to make sure you two stay in contact when I'm gone, to which Betsy replied, You don't need to worry about your father and me.

I agreed, but Stella's effort made me feel loved.

After Stella's graduation, Betsy and I bemoaned her decision to move to LA every chance we got with her, but even so we somehow got suckered into buying my mother's used perfectly maintained light blue Nissan Sentra for six hundred dollars each so Stella could have a car. She's enrolled at Santa Monica City College with plans to transfer to UCLA, and she'd lined up a room in an apartment through a Facebook friend she'd never met in person. That was her mother's big worry, but I'd met enough people online to know not to worry, to know that you can tell a lot about someone by what they post and who their friends are.

Jared wears these yoga shorts he purchased from Lululemon. Not quite as tight as a speedo, and I have to admit they look nice on him, showing off his thighs. And they're more versatile than my spandex, especially since we're getting brunch after our ride. I sip my water bottle. Jared has a coffee holder on his bike, so he drinks his coffee from a fancy-looking travel mug.

So the first time you met Betsy, you were naked on your knees?

No, don't be crass. I met her at least an hour before that. And we were standing, I say with such a straight face that Jared cackles.

He says, This just changes everything about her.

What do you mean?

Do you think they swing? He asks dramatically, but I know he's playing.

I doubt it, but I try never to assume, I say not intending to sound so intense.

Of course, of course, Jared says, stiffening a bit. But clearly Betsy's gotta a kinky streak I didn't pick up on.

How can you *pick up on* a person's kinky side?

I'm kind of like an amatuer sexual empath. You should know this.

Damn, you sound like Stella with your fancy vocabulary.

She's a smart one, my homie.

Jared loves to call me *my homie*. I regret telling him that Jason had given me a nickname. He hated Jason's choice of JG. He said, I like homie.

I said, That's like calling me dude.

He said, I know. And you are. You're my dude. My homie. And he hugged me.

Now Jared disembarks from his bike and leans it against the railing. I can tell he's wanting some information and won't stop until he gets it out of me. We've been here before.

But seriously, he says. How'd you and Betsy end up together? Meaning on your knees in front of a cock together?

It was my senior year. I was taking a class at a community college all the way across town from East San Jose. I took it there to get away from my neighborhood. I pause for a second. I close my eyes and remember: San Jose. The heat during July and August. The wide streets and low houses and infrequent trees. The corner stores and the candy I loved to buy for fifty cents after school: Chick-O-Sticks and Dinosaur Eggs. The neighborhood at dusk, running wild with other kids. The excitement of getting in a fight. The threat of returning home to find my father.

Jared says, You wanted to get away from everyone who might know you. I understand.

Sometimes Jared's ability to understand what I mean despite what I'm saying both shocks and bothers me.

Right, I say, Yes. True. That's the exact reason. Someday I'll tell you more about my jailbird father and Christian mother.

But not today.

Absolutely not.

Understood.

So, yes. I could have gone to Evergreen College, the school everyone from my neighborhood goes to, but West Valley it was. Anyway, I'd been with a few women before, but not really any men. I wanted to. I just didn't know how.

I pause, sip on my water bottle that makes those awkward gurgling sounds.

I say, I met this totally fine guy in my stats class. He invites me to this party. He's like, *It's intimate,* and winks. I'm like, *How intimate?* I think that was my first sexual proposition. Pretty damn forward for a young man of eighteen. The guy's like, *There's different rooms for various forms of intimacy.* And then he smiles. God, nice teeth and a nice mouth are my kryptonite.

Jared smiles.

Fuck you, I say.

He laughs. Keep going. I'm enjoying this.

So I'm there, and he introduces me to some of his friends. Then he introduces me to Betsy. She smiles and puts her arms around Lincoln and me at the same time.

Damn, Betsy. But wait. Your first cock was hanging from a guy named Lincoln?

Believe me, it wasn't hanging.

He pushes me, and I continue, We drink wine all up close on a couch. We smoke a little. Betsy asks if I want to join them later. I say yes. At some point Lincoln—

With the non-hanging penis, Jared interrupts.

Yes, the very same. We have ourselves a playful little threesome that is so smooth I think every threesome must be like this.

Wrong. Jared smirks.

Right, I agree. So anyway, at some point Lincoln returns to the party. Betsy and I lie next to each other. She said something like, *Juan, it's been such a pleasure meeting you,* and reached out to shake my hand. I laughed and shook her hand, and she said, *You have a wonderful laugh.* And I said, *You have a wonderful smile,* and the rest is history.

What do you mean? Did she get pregnant like the next day?

Basically. We kept hanging out and hooking up. Lincoln was, as it turned out, a bit of a smarmy dude.

Unctuous, as Stella would say, Jared adds.

I shake my head and say, So we stopped hanging out with Lincoln soon after, and Betsy and I enjoyed each other. We fooled around with others, but when we both got into Cal, we decided to move in together—and then she got pregnant at the end of summer. We still had a non-monogamous thing for most of our relationship, but you know how things go.

Yes. People stop smiling as much as they did when they first met.

That's an interesting way to say it.

We are facing Lake Merritt, looking out across the water. The path is packed today with cyclists and runners, some people holding hands and others holding leashes connected to various breeds of dogs. I push the thought of Mr. Dog out of my head by saying, It used to stink on this bridge.

The whole of Lake Merritt used to stink. But the one good thing about white people moving in—they don't want anything to stink.

And now you sound like a racist, I tease. I turn around and face Laney campus. I had hoped Stella would enroll there instead of moving down to LA. No matter how big our familia is, how good and loving, I remind myself, people need to find their own way, need to learn for themselves.

Jared says, Crazy she's leaving tomorrow. You ready?

I am, I say. Are you ready for these stairs?

I hop on my bike and proceed to the Cleveland Cascade just up the path, a hundred thirty-nine steps that everybody tackles for exercise. I mean everybody. Crossfit classes lifting their knees high, teachers barking at them to *move move move*. Determined old ladies in colorful flowing trousers and floral patterned shirts and visored hats. Shockingly fast sprinters in all shades of neon with earbuds and sunglasses, and then people like me and Jared, the noncommitted, the dabblers, the ones clearly here on a lark.

We walk up and down in silence. I can see Jared thinking about something, but unlike him, I don't have the ability to read others' silence. I worry I said the wrong thing.

The one thing we are not dabblers about is brunch. We gorge on huevos rancheros and guacamole on the patio of Doña Tomás, one of the original restaurants in Temescal before the uber hipster scene exploded all over the neighborhood. Betsy and I used to take Stella here because the place lets kids run amok.

I tell Jared this, and he elaborates. The first restaurant in the area was that catfish place across the street—now gone, sadly—and the Ethiopian restaurant, Asmara.

Yes, and that deli. Genova's, I say.

Those sandwiches, though? Jared says.

I hate how things change. I really do.

So on that note, I've been thinking.

I brace myself.

How do you feel about you and me? Let's check in.

Here in public?

Jared says, I said check in, not brawl. Is there something emotionally painful you need to say? Because yes, we can wait if you need to.

No, not that. I just…

I didn't know what *I just*. I wish that Jared would intuit what *I just* means and share it with me, because something is there.

I say, It's an intense day. I'm not sure what I'm feeling night now.

I understand. You're right. Thanks for reminding me. Let me just say this. I'm ready. For more. I'm ready for bigger things. Which is not to say that all these things need to happen now. But I'm ready. You think on that and talk to me when you have had some time to process your daughter leaving.

I nod and say, Thank you for understanding. I will talk to you about all these things when I can.

That's all I can ask for. He reaches out and squeezes my shoulder.

That night, Betsy and I sit at her table, made from one solid hewn slab of redwood, with Stella. I didn't invite Jared, and Betsy didn't invite Stan. We had hugged and cooked and and shared stories of her childhood. It felt like the beginning, when we were a bubble of domesticity, when we first had Stella and created something entirely new. A family.

Betsy says, What are you going to miss the most about the Bay?

Stella thinks.

I add, Besides us, of course.

Yes, you two. But not much else, to be honest.

Really? I ask.

Really. I mean, besides you two and a few friends, who else is there?

Betsy couldn't say her parents, Stella's grandparents, who had moved to Arizona shortly after Betsy graduated from high school and happily wrote holiday cards with money tucked inside as their main form of communication with Stella. I couldn't say my parents —my father in prison and my mother in Salinas. Despite the latter's stuffed animal gifts, we barely saw her.

Food. That's what I'll miss. Good food.

They got granola in LA, I say.

And just like that, the dinner ends. Stella stands and walks to my chair. She hugs me so deeply and tightly. I kiss her on the cheeks. I hold her out from me. I bite my bottom lip. Stella bites her lip, teasing me.

That's your angry face, she says.

I'm not angry.

He's just emotional, Betsy says and reaches around to hug both of us.

We did it, Juan. Our little flour quesadilla.

Don't call me that, Stella says.

But it was the perfect nickname for you, I say.

When I was a baby, perhaps, but not now.

Ok, honey, Betsy says.

We continue to hug until Stella's phone vibrates and she extricates herself and blows us kisses as she saunters down the hall to her room.

Text me on the drive, I shout.

That's illegal, she shouts back.

Not *while* you're driving!

I look at Betsy. She says sternly, That car better make it. Otherwise, you're driving down to get her.

I got to work tomorrow, I say.

I got work tomorrow too, she shoots back.

If it were any other time, I might get irritated at how she tells me what to do. But not now.

And the next day, Stella's gone. Just like that.

The next month is a blur of plunging into work and spending more time at Nicks and biking around Lake Merritt and running those goddamn stairs, sometimes with Jared, sometimes with the old ladies in the early afternoon before school lets out. And there are dinners at restaurants, sometimes with Jared, sometimes alone. I try not to lean too hard on Jared. I resist his desire to be there. I set up hard boundaries. I fidget around the empty house. I move my work station into Stella's room. I try to establish a new pattern. Ritual is my life. It helps with everything—including avoidance of serious conversations and passing the time.

It also helps that I call Stella every Tuesday and Thursday before I go to Nicks, where I watch A's highlights since the Warriors are over and drink sparkly water until I have my one and only drink. Bulleit on the rocks. But beforehand, it's our father/daughter date. It's the way we stay connected since we can't see each other. She tells me about the assignments in her classes, living in Santa Monica, and the strange absence of techies crowding coffee shops. She gets a job at a health-food store, where she meets her new boyfriend, Byron.

Byron? I repeated when she told me.

Yes.

And he's your boss?

No, more my supervisor.

That's better?

Not really. But it's not an issue.

Why? I asked like she could infer all I meant from the one word: Are you safe? Are you lonely? Are you homesick? Are you sure?

Why not? she replied.

I couldn't argue with that.

The one issue is the car. It broke down a month into her new life. I don't know shit about cars, and we don't trust anyone in LA to tell her whether the car is worth fixing. So now it sits in front of her apartment complex.

What should I do with it? She asks me.

I feel accused.

Did you text your *abuela* about it?

It's not her fault, Dad.

I know, I say, but I so desperately wanted to blame her.

Can your new boyfriend look at it? I ask.

I can look at it, but that doesn't mean I can fix it, Dad.

I say, I know. That's not what I meant. I meant does he know about cars.

He's an English major, she says.

So was I, I say. What's that got to do with it?

Exactly, she says. It has everything to do with it. And so I guess this is as good a time as any to tell you that Byron is living with me till the end of the semester. I'm assuming that's cool, or should we get married?

No, I say immediately.

No to moving in, or no to marriage?

Both. You just met this person.

82

Dad, you're the last person I expected to hear that comment from. Look at you and mom.

Right, and look at us now. Look at me and Jared. We took our time.

Are you guys moving in?

No.

Why not? It's been like over a year, right?

Because there's no rush.

After that much time, it hardly seems like rushing.

This is not about Jared. When you're nineteen, it's rushing. You've only been dating him for what?

Almost three months.

Don't you need to sow your wild granola?

She giggles, and I remember her as a jubilant toddler running wildly up and down our sidewalk.

Stella, I say.

What?

Do you even love him?

Who said anything about that? But sure. I guess, she says.

You guess?

Yes, I guess. I guess I love him for now. How's that, Dad? Anyway, he's paying half my rent, so it'll save you and mom some money. Look, I understand it's hard to support me, and I appreciate it, but I can't even get the car fixed. He's a good guy. You're going to have to trust me on this one, Dad.

It sounds really serious.

Well, I'm not adding him to our group text, so just relax.

She gets off the phone. I try to sit with what I'm feeling. I'm appalled by the idea of her adding someone to our Big Familia. I get on the computer, and an hour later I text Big Familia: I got you a Triple A card. Just go ahead and get the car towed to a mechanic. Call a couple first and see which one you like. Trust your instincts. I'll pay for it.

Ok, thanks, she replies.

Good papa, texts Betsy.

But I don't feel good. I feel mistrustful. Suspicious. I feel like I don't need anything more. I don't want anything more. I feel like I'm about to lose something, like everything I have isn't where I thought it was.

8

What *Belay* Really Means

Everyone else in my life seems to be getting more serious in their relationships. Stella and Byron in LA. Betsy finally announced her engagement to Stan. I even think Bob and Rachel now cohabitate. The person closest to me who's still unattached, I realize with some shock, has to be Jason with his greasy hair and dirty fingernails. He certainly appears single to me, but we've never actually talked about dating. Sports and politics, but never our lovers, never the things that matter most.

I have commented to Jared a few times lately that maybe things are moving too fast. I don't know if I want more, or less, or nothing at all. I don't know if I'm ready. Jared continually lets me know he is by being communicative and compromising and open to how I feel, by sharing his feelings and being willing to take me and all my baggage into consideration. It's not that those things aren't appealing, but talking about those things isn't appealing.

Maybe I'm a victim of empty nest syndrome, something I admit only to myself—wrestling with the need to rediscover who I am, or to think about only my wants. Regardless, I'm feeling the need to protect myself, and because of that I've avoided any serious talk with Jared for weeks. We have actually settled into a pretty specific weekend routine: Friday we chill and watch Netflix since Jared is usually tired from the work week. I cook while he searches for and then offers up three viewing options. We have fun debating, yet usually choose the one that's closest to Marvel movies: special powers and action and sublimated teenage desire.

Saturday is our play day: coffee and breakfast, biking, and a dinner out.

Sunday we check in regularly—which usually consists of him bemoaning the stress of the upcoming week and me complaining about Stella—and run errands.

Domestic bliss and denial: the makings of all great partnerships.

But today one of those pointless little things happens that breaks shit wide open, like the underwear on the floor.

We spent the afternoon at my place, and as we were leaving, Jared realized he forgot his iPad. I grudgingly got off the bike to unlock the door.

Why are you angry? Jared asks. You know, if I had a key, I could just do it myself.

I ignore him and rush upstairs, but he won't let it go.

Juan, so there are a couple things I've been thinking about, he says minutes later, coasting alongside me.

He says, It's not huge, but it's important to me. First, I want to have some space at your apartment, and I'd like to provide you space in mine. In fact, I'd like to exchange keys officially.

Like a key-exchange ceremony, I say, trying to be light.

Fuck rings, Jared says. I've always believed commitment is a key. I can get you a cute custom key, if you want: a Warriors key, or one with jumping dolphins.

Can't we just let things happen? I shout, the evening chill making each exhale visible.

There's a silence, as though he's taken aback by my words or my volume or both. Then he raises his own voice. Some things you need to plan. Some words require action, he says and sprints past me.

I don't respond. I feel childish in my disappointment. I wanted him to say, *Yes, of course, Juan. We can do what you want.*

I let go of the handlebars, trying to distract myself, to feel how the nighttime moves around me. My cheeks flush in the cold, my body moving quickly forward. I see Jared in front of me. I race on past him and never want to stop.

In the morning, Jared and I are sitting in his bed. The best thing about his bedroom is the way the early light floods in from the large window above our heads and warms the opposite wall.

I say, So before we exchange keys, I was thinking maybe we should open up for a month or two and see others to make sure.

Jared snorts and looks at me, half smiling, and then he realizes I'm serious. I watch him pull himself together: sit upright a little more, stretch out his legs, and shake the blankets up and down a few times.

Juan, I am not opposed to opening up. But I am opposed to do-ing it to *make sure.* If that is the reason, my homie, I think you're being a real dick, and I don't use that word lightly.

I can hear in his tone that he's holding back his anger. I scoff and explain, No, not make sure. I guess I just need to feel a little autonomous. A little free. Right now. Does that make sense?

He says, Thank you for being honest. But listen, you can't keep avoiding the difficult things. You want everything smooth and easy. That just doesn't happen. You have to make them smooth and easy. You have to trust your gut, your heart. It's been over a year. If you still need to make sure, then you're not sure.

I close my eyes. I try to feel my gut, my heart. I try to read what they are saying. I then feel Jared kiss my mouth. I don't move. I feel the softness of his lips and the weight of his body leaning on mine.

Jared says, I love you, but I deserve to be in a relationship with someone who wants to be in the same kind of relationship. What does the word relationship mean to you, Juan?

He asks this but clearly doesn't expect an answer. Standing, he straightens his tighty non-whitey underwear. I stare at his legs, the sparse coils of black hair.

Jared walks to the bathroom. I smooth out the bedsheets.

After a minute, he leans back in the room, toothbrush in mouth, looking at me.

I feel examined.

Jared returns to the bathroom.

I hear him spit and rinse and spit and rinse. He repeats this six times. Each time the squeak of the faucet being turned on and then off makes me more on edge.

He enters the room and states, Look, I am going to cuddle you for a few minutes. Then I'm going to leave. Stay for a while, if you want, think about what it means for a relationship to work. You think about what this means to you for the next month or two. If you want to hook up with someone, do it—as long as you prioritize our time, keep it safe, and never lie to me about it if I ask you. We can hang out when it feels right. Then, hopefully, you'll be sure.

He reaches to my chest. His hands are cold and damp, but I don't pull away. He keeps his hands on my body and stares at me without blinking, a challenge, a dare.

I want to say something, want to answer his question with clarity and honesty. I want words that capture everything I feel and am afraid of. As I breathe in to speak, he says, No, don't. Just come here. He pulls me to him.

Normally when we cuddle, I wrap around him. I am able to lean into him if I get cold or roll away when I get too hot. But now he nudges me to turn over and spoons me. I lie there wondering how the term *spooning* came to be, rather than *cupping* or *curling*. It feels wonderful. Like we understand each other without having to speak. Like there can be no confusion in our actions.

* * *

Three weeks go by, and Jared and I hang out only Saturday nights. It's light and serious simultaneously, like we don't know if it's the last time but we still want all the things: intimacy, conversation, hot sex.

When Betsy and I broke up, it was quick. Like a door shutting. Like a slap. Stella was twelve. We really didn't do much together then besides parent her. We hung out with a few of Stella's friends' parents, most of whom we met at parks and soccer games and birthday parties, but besides that, we each just found pleasure in separate things, things that got in the way before we noticed they had gotten in the way. Betsy and I stopped having "parties," as she liked to call the nights we shared lovers, sometimes a woman, mostly a man. Partly we stopped because it felt more risky as Stella grew up. It was easier to take turns going out. We still slept regularly with each other, our sex familiar and comforting, but rote. I had become effective in my work/time management, which allowed me to get distracted by my many serial non-monogamous relations with sexy man after butch woman after bottomy boy. Betsy became more involved in her design business, which took her to community meetings and public offices and government buildings. She had a couple of affairs with married men that ended badly, but she was a mover and shaker, playing a role in bringing about Oakland's growing economic desirability. She was determined and focused and articulate and refused to let that old-boy network stop whatever she was doing.

I think we both loved our setup. We each had a good partner, a coparent, a double income, a friend. I told this to Betsy the night she said she wanted a divorce.

Exactly, she said. I love you, but we're partners in a mostly platonic sense.

That's a bad thing? I asked.

It's not, but I want more. I need more. I feel myself stuck in this pattern, this routine.

Again, that's not a bad thing, is it?

It can be. It is for me. Maybe in the future I'd love a pattern like the one we are in. But as a woman, I feel it's important to demand more of myself, to not settle, because it's so easy to settle.

If you stay with me you're settling? That is pretty fucked up.

No, if I choose not to listen to my deepest intuition, then I'll be settling.

I couldn't argue with that. I knew exactly what she meant. It was the reason I told her when we decided to keep Stella that I couldn't stop seeing men, but I could promise to commit to our relationship.

What about Stella? I asked Betsy, feeling suddenly panicky, abandoned. What do you need from me to stay?

Stella has nothing to do with our decisions, and actually I want Stella to see us prioritizing ourselves in loving and noncompromising and healthy ways. She reached out and put her hands on me. What I need from you? I actually need you to love me and trust me and let me go. She said, I'm your family. I'll always be there for you. I'll always be your partner. Perhaps this is something you need as well, but you just can't see it yet.

I wanted so badly to snap at her. How dare she tell me what I could or couldn't see? I stood up. I said, Fine. I'll give you a month to change your mind. If after a month you still want a divorce, I won't stop you.

A month later Betsy moved her stuff to an apartment two blocks away. Betsy, Stella, and I spent one final evening together at our King Street apartment, soon to be just my apartment. I had read in a library book that ceremonies, especially ones that involve the children, even friends, helped them cope with parental separation. That night we each lit a long wood matchstick and pressed the flames to a candlewick at the same time. Once the votive was lit, we walked to Betsy's new apartment. In retrospect, the ritual was important to all of us. In retrospect, perhaps Betsy was correct.

But here I am again: wondering if I'm not seeing something,

wondering what things in my life really mean. I decide I need to go on some dates. To help my clarity, I tell myself.

I set up a profile on a free dating site one Friday evening, accompanied by some nice smooth bourbon. It's like a date with myself. Feels dangerous, drinking on a day I don't normally drink.

For the self-summary I write: *Luddite working as a web designer, which is to say I struggle with self-contempt but I'm ok with compromise.* For the life description, I write: *parent of one daughter who attends college in LA, avid exercise avoider, but I like to bike.*

Perhaps the bourbon isn't helping, I realize.

As I peruse people's profiles, I discover a secret language. The number of people who want *belay partners* to rock climb is stunning. So many that I initially think *belay* is a code word for something I clearly haven't tried. Literally three out of four profiles mention rock climbing as a pastime. When people say they *like to laugh,* it's code for *I'm fun and don't take things too seriously. I don't watch TV* is code for *I'm selective and discerning.* Once this is implied, people then usually list a few exceptions—respectable TV shows with just one or two trashy ones thrown in.

The more profiles I read, the sparser my own becomes, the less I want to say, or the more I want to be direct, so my answer to what I'm looking for ends up simply: *Looking for temporary distraction. Looking to forget. Looking to get laid.*

Shockingly, I quickly set up three dates. Two of them are with women, one with a man, and none of my dates has a name beginning with the letter J. It's a good omen.

First up is Amanda, five foot three, in grad school, works as a high-end food-server, favorite book is Orwell's *1984*. She suggests meeting in downtown Oakland but not at one of the new restaurants or bars. She doesn't want to see coworkers or regular customers. I suggest Giant Burger on 22nd and Telegraph. When we approach each other, I realize I don't know how to greet her. I reach out to shake hands but immediately feel too businesslike, so when

I grip her hand, I pull her toward me and into a hug. I feel her resist for a second, then give in. She smells like gardenias and looks like a newscaster—thin, well dressed, with straightened hair. We sit on stools that seem to be stuffed with something horrifically uncomfortable, like rocks, and I continually shift throughout our conversation.

She begins, I should have said I don't eat meat.

We look at the menu, and there is absolutely nothing without meat except the French fries.

She says, I have some carrots in my purse.

I say, I'll share fries with you.

She says, Ok, but like I have disappointed her, then she takes out the carrots out and begins to eat them, not offering any to me.

When the fries come, I proceed to nervously eat most of the basket while she periodically salts one fry at a time and dips it precisely one third of the way into a little container of mustard.

Trying to be funny, I say, Who likes mustard on fries?

I do, she says.

I say, It must be an acquired taste. I smile after I say it, conveying *I'm not being serious.*

She says, Not if you like mustard.

At this point I know the date is a failure. I fidget through another thirty minutes until she says she has to run. We shake. Neither of us tries for a hug.

The second date, Mark, works in public relations, five foot five, favorite book *Moby Dick,* which I am sure is code for *cock*, so I am both apprehensive and horny, which is never a good combination. It doesn't matter though. He never shows up at the Green Nut, an organic Thai restaurant. While I wait, I order two rounds of coconut milk, which come in the actual coconuts with colorful straws. I spend an hour palming their scratchy hardness and scraping the soft white meat from their insides, sucking it up and into my mouth.

The third date is with Maggie, five foot six, likes to rock climb, favorite book the Harry Potter series. She has a child, so I figure we'll have something to talk about. We set it up for Sunday evening, but Maggie texts at three in the afternoon to say she's at this divey sports bar called George and Walt's, drinking with friends.

Come on down now, she says.

I bike there to find her with a couple—the woman a large blond with a face like she just woke up. She's Maggie's best friend, I'm told. The guy looks disturbingly like my Jared—thin, black, well dressed, small clean dreads.

They're all feeling good, code for *hammered.*

They're so drunk they make me not want to drink, so I order a bubbly water, and they all stare at my glass. Clearly, getting a non-alcoholic drink with three people already drunk is not the best way to ease into a conversation. I can tell that Maggie regrets inviting me. She'd apparently forgotten that she's actually never met me. I watch her trying to pull herself together, to be her normal self, sitting upright and bundling her hands in her lap like a small animal.

I want to pet them. Instead I find the little black straw to my bubbly water with my mouth and take a big sip. I feel like Frankie, which helps me relax. I ask, So where's your son today? Did you leave him at home to give yourself a break for an hour? I smile as I say this, conveying *I am joking, trying to be funny, one parent to another.*

She immediately starts huffing and puffing, fanning her face with her small animal hands like she's fighting tears or shooing away insects. The blond says, Oh baby, oh baby, come here, and hugs her.

Then the blonde gives the guy who's my ex-lover's twin that look only couples can give, a mix of reproach, like *handle this, you asshole,* and commiseration, like *can you believe this happened?*

The guy jumps up. He cups my elbow, his hand warm and slightly moist. He pulls me to the front of the bar.

I think you'd best leave, he whispers. Not a threat. More like revealing a secret.

I say, Thanks for being straight with me.

He says, There isn't any other way.

I scoff and say, I wish that were true.

I walk away considering how many ways there are to not be straight with someone. I think of how often we say something other than what we are trying to say, how our words so often fail us. Like when we say *hey, this isn't working,* instead of *I'm scared that I like you too much,* or we say *looking for a belay partner* instead of *will you please, please just hold me.*

9

Cracks You Cannot Feel

When my cell phone rings, I hear it in my bag in the hallway. It's the sound of a car horn, meaning it's Betsy. I'm focused and content working in my new office in Stella's old room. I've kept her bulletin board up, with all her collected memorabilia: clipper cards, digitally printed photos, some artwork. I haven't repainted or moved her furniture, except for adding my small computer desk. In fact, I realize, it's still basically Stella's room.

I ignore the phone, and it stops, then a second later rings again. I go dig it out. Hello, I say.

Hi, Betsy says, relief in her voice. Juan, have you talked to Stella?

No, I say, becoming aware of my heart beating, beating, beating.

She's fine, but she's in a situation, Betsy says.

Betsy. Tell me what's up.

She says, I should let her. I think she wants to tell you. She's fine, but.

And then Betsy starts to sob. I have not heard Betsy cry in so long, I'm unsure what is happening. She got all teary at Stella's graduation, but there is a definite difference between that sound and this sound. She didn't shed tears when we officially divorced, signing papers in a mediator's office, nor on the day she moved out, nor, come to think of it, when we got married. Not even at the birth of our daughter. The last time she cried in front of me was when she told me she was pregnant.

I was nineteen, and she was twenty. We sat on our bed in an apartment shared with a few other San Jose transplants living in West Oakland. My dad was about to be incarcerated, my mother about to move back to Salinas, and Betsy's parents had relocated to Tucson. We both knew we were all the other had.

What's the matter? I remember asking, seeing how horrified she looked. I worried I'd done something wrong.

She said flatly, I'm so sorry.

I shook my head with growing apprehension.

I've ruined everything. I'm pregnant.

I quickly thought back to the last time we shared a male lover. It had been a while. I pictured his face, his belly, his cock. But I knew it wasn't him. I sat still, weathering a massive desire to blame her. She waited for me to respond, tears rolling down her face, but making no sound. I felt something give. I said simply and with complete naiveté, We are going to be badass parents, and then I hugged her, feeling arrogant and determined.

Then she let it out. She bawled.

I want to react to her tears now the way I did back then, but I feel panicky, scared, so I hang up on Betsy. I hit my daughter's name in my phone. When Stella answers, she has this sluggish sound to her voice.

Your mother told me to call you, I say.

Yes, she says. I asked her to.

Well, I am. I'm calling.

Dad. I'm pregnant.

My first reaction is relief. My mind races through the things I fear: car accidents or arrests for drugs. I fixate for a minute on the boyfriend. Anger surges through me.

Dad, she says again. I hear the nervousness in her voice. I realize that's why she sounds weird. I understand she needs something from me. That she's waiting for something from me.

I say, Who's the father?

I hear her make a sharp sound, like she's been slapped.

I'm sorry, I say. I know it's Byron. I didn't mean it that way. But what did he do when you told him?

What does it matter what he did, Dad? She says.

I know. I know, I say, trying to think through my next words. I really just want to hold her. I want to pull her into me, to feel the warmth of her body.

She begins to speak, but I cut her off. I say, I am so proud of you. For all the work and sacrifices you've made to get where you are. You've made some tough choices, and that experience will help make this tough choice. You need to choose yourself. Not some guy, and definitely not a baby. Not now.

Dad, she says. I think I've ruined everything.

When Betsy had spoken that same phrase, I hadn't believed it, but now I see she was right. Or not right, but I see how different things would have been if we had chosen differently. If someone had set us straight.

I say, You will ruin your life if you don't get rid of it. You'll always be connected to this guy. To this child. To this choice.

I hear her breathing in that way people do when they are trying not to show emotion. It's a cooing sound. Like she's warming up her voice. Like she might sing.

I say, It's not too late to fix this. You can come home. You can move back in.

She shouts, Dad, listen to me. I'm already three months. I am keeping the child. I have Byron. I am not coming home.

I'm silent. Stunned.

She says, I was just hoping that you'd be happy, and that I wouldn't need to give up on everything else because of this.

I say as calmly as I can, Stella, you've only been there for four months. What the fuck were you thinking? Stop being a stupid child.

And now it comes. She makes those guttural sounds. She is clearly not even listening anymore, but I keep talking.

I say, Don't you get it? This changes everything.

She screams, Fine! So what? It doesn't matter. Things will still be ok.

I know she wants me to agree. Tell her that yes, things will be ok. And I want to say it. I want to soothe her, to reassure her. I want her not to worry. But I feel angry at her and feel sad for her at the same time, so instead I say, No. Things are not going to be ok. They are going to be hard. But it's your stupid fucking choice. And I disconnect from her.

I lose my shit a little. I walk in circles through the house, which feels small and cluttered. I text Jared—fuck calling him—and confirm our date tomorrow night. I decide I'm going to purge everything from this cramped house, and I start in Stella's room. Almost immediately I discover our Nativity set in a box that's labeled in Stella's cute little handwriting: *keep*.

We never did much for the holidays, but Stella always liked to get a little tree. After the divorce, Betsy and I tried to alternate years: you do Christmas, I'll do Thanksgiving, and so on, but Stella somehow got both of us to feel like shitty parents if we lacked the festive spirit, so each year we ventured together to Delancey Street Christmas Trees and bought a two-foot fir—one for each of us—from an ex-con. See, Stella would say, we're helping people out, which is the true purpose of the holiday.

My mother gave me the Nativity set when Betsy and I got our first place together. It was hand painted, made from wood, with donkeys and a Mary and a Joseph and a cradle and a little baby

Jesus. Each year, Stella would spend so much time setting it up perfectly, and I would play jokes on her and move baby Jesus secretly—so he rode the donkey or was under the cradle, or I'd put the donkey in the cradle and baby Jesus would be trailing behind Joseph. It was our game.

I sit on the floor and set up the figures just the way Stella would, and the only thing that's missing are blinking lights, which for years I have refused to have in my house. Suddenly it's all I can do to keep from bawling because I don't have any. I stand by the light switch and flick the overhead light on and off to see if that does something. It doesn't.

I call my mother and tell her I'm coming over tomorrow.

In the morning I drive my 1978 Mercedes to my mom's. It's the car I taught Stella to drive in, despite her initial refusal to learn both because it was a stick shift and looked like a hoopty car. She held out until she was seventeen and the only one of her friends who couldn't drive. It also helped that we put her on an Uber limit, meaning Uber only in emergencies. Like being stranded. Like someone too drunk to drive. Not like *I don't want to ride the bus or BART*. She refused to practice driving where anyone she might possibly know could see her, so one morning on a school day, we headed to Golden Gate Fields in Albany. In their massive and empty parking lot, she spent three hours driving circles and figure eights and racing forward and screeching to a stop. At the only hill on the lot, I made her stop and start the car again and again. She cried and laughed and yelled at me. I yelled and cajoled and reassured and teased and shared stories of me learning to drive with my father, which are the only stories of my father I care to share.

She made me tell her more at Denny's, her reward for learning to drive, the closest thing to fast food I'd allow, and something we never did in Berkeley. I said, When I was a little boy, he would sit me in his lap and push on the gas pedal, telling me he no longer steered the car. That it was all me. I loved it, but he always scared me. Like we'd be about to roll up to a stop light, and he'd ask me—now remember, I'm like eight—he'd ask, *Are you pressing the brake?* knowing I wasn't pressing the brake. I didn't even know where the fucking brake was. He'd say, *Mijo, you better stop the car. Mijo, Mijo!* he'd scream louder and louder. I would panic and let go of the wheel and cover my face. Then the car would stop, and he'd laugh and laugh.

That's so mean, Dad, Stella said.

That's my father. So yes, he gave me a few lessons later, let me practice around our neighborhood, and then one day I'm walking out of school and my father is standing at the gate. My mom's little light blue Nissan is there, parked half on the sidewalk, half off. I could never drive his car, which was a Chevy Nova, not all fixed up, but still. He waved me over. My friends were all afraid of him because he had this shaved head and a thick mustache. When you saw it, he had it all trimmed, but when I was a kid, it was like Zapata's mustache. Anyway, he's all, *I need you to drive your mother's car home. I got plans.* He throws me the keys and steps into this other car, and it screeches out of there. The security guy at our school comes up and says, *You have to move this car now.* My friends all start howling and cheering me on.

Did you have a license? Sella asks.

I was like fifteen. I didn't even have a permit.

That's crazy. I don't believe you.

It was the late nineties in east San Jose. You could do anything.

What happened?

I learned to drive.

I'm all nostalgic by the time I hit the freeway. Driving always does this to me. Makes me sappy. Emotional. I love my Mercedes because it's so slow and there's no radio, and so I just let go and chill. I drive the two hours to my mom's.

Juanito, my mother says with this quiet happiness when I arrive. Come in, come in.

The house is a squat '50s-style ranch, immaculately clean with shag carpet throughout and a few display cases full of religious figurines, including my favorite, a porcelain replica of La Pietà that belonged to my abuela. I remember holding it as a child when I went to visit her. She would sit me on her lap and let me hold it like it was more precious than gold, and she'd make me promise that someday I'd go see the real thing in Rome. I was fascinated by it. It had these superfine cracks that spider-webbed across the opalescent glazing. The look on the face of dying Jesus was both agony and pleasure, the look on the Virgin's face one of such resolve and love. When my abuela passed away, that was the only thing I wanted, but my mother refused to give it to me, saying it was for believers only.

I walk around the living room while my mother makes coffee. I find La Pietà on the top shelf of a glass cabinet. She hands a cup to me, and I sip, and it's perfect. I think of Jared, how I want to make him watch and learn from her. I think about how he'd probably also try to have sex with me in this house because it'd be so dirty and hot. Strange how I can both miss and get angry with him when he isn't even here.

We sit at the dining room table with a large wooden crucifix firmly in the center. She sits across from me. Her hair is thick and full and cut short. Almost hip, not that she cares at all about being hip. She cares about practicality. She wears a cream sweater, puffy and warm. Her lips red as ever. I can see the red stain on the rim of the coffee mug.

Have you talked with my father? I ask.

You know he wants nothing to do with me. But I pray for him.

We're still not on the visiting list?

I don't even check any more.

And you, Mama?

I'm fine, but enough about me. I assume you are still single?

I smile when she refers to being queer as single. I don't think I would have ever told my mom I was queer if she hadn't ardently preached such homophobic shit to Stella as a child. When I finally did, she said she already knew and had prayed for me. Then she kissed my forehead and walked out of the room.

I say, I'm not single. I'm seeing Jared. Jared is my partner.

I sound like I'm convincing myself of something, which bothers me.

Here. I set the box with the Nativity on her table.

She slides it to her and says, I'll hold on to it for her. You never know when she'll want it for her own family.

Well then you might not be holding on to it for too long. Stella's pregnant. I say it in a way that implies we can both talk shit about her, but my mom breaks into a wide, open-mouthed smile.

Oh, Juan. I am so happy for you. You must be so proud, she says.

You heard that's she's pregnant? She's three months along. She's been in LA for four months. Do the math.

Don't be gross, she chides. It's natural and God's plan. She's young. She's beautiful. She's going to be an amazing mother.

You don't even know the father.

She shrugs. Fathers. You should know you can't trust them.

Despite myself, I laugh. I ask, Why are you happy for her, but you were never supportive of Betsy and me?

And how is Betsy?

She's good, but why, Mama?

She places both palms on the table with the coffee mug between them. Gracefully and with purpose.

You were right. I was wrong. I should have been more supportive. Maybe you would still be together.

No, I doubt that, but what's gotten into you? I ask, trying to hide my shock.

She sips her coffee and says, I see so many people at the church who are unhappy. So many people alone. You know we're a sanctuary church now for immigrants. My goodness, the stories they tell us about leaving the people they love behind. Their kids. Their parents. Their husbands and wives. I guess I no longer see a point in denying yourself the company of someone you love or care about. Someone you call family.

I stare at her.

I don't like your choices, she continues. But I love you. I want you to be happy. I want to see you more often.

I spend the whole day with her, helping her with odds and ends, trying to connect the stoic, distant person who raised me with the person before me now who seems remorseful but not broken. A person who realized something and then made a change. It's both inspiring and frustrating.

When I leave, she says, Here. Take this. Maybe it will remind you of God's love more than the Nativity did. She hands me La Pietà. I rub my fingertips across the surface and close my eyes, trying to feel the minute cracks in the porcelain, but I feel absolutely nothing. It's so beautifully smooth.

That evening I ask Jared to just come to my house. I ask him to bring a bottle of wine and some pizza. I ask him like everything was normal and nothing had changed.

After our first glass and a couple slices, as I'm enjoying that sweet, excited energy we share when we haven't seen each other in a while, he asks, Are you ok? You seem a bit . . . desperate's the wrong word, but something's going on.

I want to tell him that I'm fine, that things are actually good, so we can just enjoy the present. But I say, No. I don't know. Things were good. I mean they are. But now everything seems fucked up. Stella's pregnant.

Jared looks at me like he's deciding how to react. He says, I can't imagine how difficult and scary this must feel, and he gets this attentive expression on his face, his *you-talk-I'll-listen* look. It irritates me because I recognize it, and I think of how many fucking times he has turned this pity-poor-Juan look on me.

He asks, What happened when you told your parents Betsy was pregnant?

I don't want to talk, but I can't help it. I say, Betsy's parents thought her life was over and told her that she was such a disappointment. When she broke the news to me, she burst out crying like it was the worst possible thing that could happen. I think she thought I was going to hate her.

And your parents? Jared asks.

I remember how I borrowed Betsy's car to drive down to San Jose. I didn't bring Betsy. I wanted to face my parents alone. Plus I needed time to figure out how I felt.

Mama, Betsy is pregnant.

She didn't stop looking through a *People* magazine at our dining room table, adorned with a wood crucifix and lace doilies and a Tupperware container with her famous spaghetti topped with one slice of American cheese.

So why should you care? she asked flatly.

Because I'm the father.

You? She looked up, stared at me blankly for a second, then she laughed—her mouth wide open and red lips curled. She laughed in disbelief.

Yes, me, I said firmly.

She closed the magazine, stood, and walked around to me. She said, And you think this is a good thing? She softly patted my face while she considered me for a long moment, and finally she spoke: Have you told your father?

I hadn't, and when I asked what time he would be home, my mother shrugged. She said, Help yourself to what's in the fridge. I'm going out.

She left, confident and carefree. Like she had someplace to be.

It was hours before I heard his Chevy Nova pulling up. I sauntered outside. He looked confused when I leaned in the passenger-side window.

You moved back already? he asked like he figured I'd be back soon enough, but not quite this soon.

No, I said. I didn't pause. Betsy's pregnant.

He turned off the idling Nova, walked around the car, and gave me a big hug. He whispered, I knew it boy. I knew you had it in you. But be careful with the white ones. They got the law on their side.

When I said Ok, he softly patted me on my face just like my mom had and said, Proud of you boy.

Juan. Juan, Jared repeats, standing in front of me, and I realize I've been completely out of it.

Sorry, I say. I'm just.

It's fine.

No, it's fine. My dad was proud of me, I say.

Probably because he thought it meant you weren't queer, Jared says.

I'm not sure how to explain my father's visible relief. It was like everything fell into order for him in that moment, everything was the way it should be. It made me disgusted with myself and yet happy. Like I was a good, good boy.

I'm suddenly exhausted and angry. I told Stella she's ruined her life, I say.

Because she's pregnant? Why would you do that?

Because she has. She's ruining it.

Jared says, Wait, do you think you ruined your life because you had Stella? Juan, you didn't tell her that, did you?

I don't respond.

Oh, Juan, you need to call her. You need to fix this.

Jared reaches out, but I lean back. I don't want to be touched. He gets this stern face, his features hardening.

He says, Don't do it, Juan.

What? I say. I feel my body tensing. I feel my jaw clenching.

He says, Juan, let me tell you a couple things about me. I was your basic middle-class black kid whose mother loved and supported him, but I still found shit to be angry about back then. I'm still dealing with that anger today. I work extremely hard to just be me and not rage about stuff I can't control or can't change. You know what I'm saying?

No, I don't. What's your point? I snap. Because I hate being lectured. I hate being babied. I hate being coddled.

He says, This is my point. There are lots of things to be pissed off about. A racist, sexist president. Kids getting killed in the neighborhood, in schools. But being cared for and having allies is not one of them. Let the people who love you hold you up. Let them soothe you.

He pulls me to him. I resist at first but then tuck my face into his armpit. I can smell his scent hiding behind the deodorant. He keeps saying, Let me, let me, over and over.

And I do. I let him hold me, and I breathe in and out a few times to center myself. But when it ends I pull away. I rise and step backward.

Jared watches me. He gets to his feet too.

It's a standoff. I see that he's frustrated. I see it in the way he begins to rub his thighs. I see that look of realization, and then of resignation. I see that he's given up.

And I'm thankful.

Juan, You have a lot going on, he says. I know this might feel like poor timing, but I think we should take a break. I think you have a lot of personal work you need to do. Without this—he gestures toward the space between us—getting in the way.

I don't say anything, but I nod.

He nods.

He walks to the door, and I watch him gather his jacket, put it on, and turn to me.

You need to handle things with Stella. Be the person I know you are.

I have a moment of indecison, of regret. I say, Jared, are you sure?

He says without hesitation, Juan, I'm sure.

10

Movie Theaters and Mistletoe

The last thing I wanted to do is become a cliché. But I was so angry.

At Stella and Betsy, because they were so giddy. Betsy went immediately to visit Stella and Byron to help them prepare for the baby. Stella and I had talked, and I said I was sorry, and I *was*, but something else was there, and Stella knew it. There was a distance.

At Jared, for not reaching out, or for being so sure about ending our relationship.

At myself, mostly, I realize—because I was lonely. Because I had so much time on my hands. Because it was the fucking holidays. Because I missed Jared. Because I wanted to drink and eat too much to quench the desire to feel full. Because I just wanted to have casual sex on my terms.

To deal with these feelings, I biked more. I worked at coffee shops rather than in the living room. I moved my office out of Stella's room. I also started attending matinee movies on Fridays to celebrate the end of the week.

It was there that I hooked up with someone. It happened in the real world and not on an app. It happened in the dark. As soon as some movie with Matt Damon started, this person sat three seats from me in an almost empty theater. This meant something, I was sure of it. I had never had anonymous sex, but I assumed there was a script to follow. I realized I had no idea how to make it happen. I felt sad, a little hurt, like I was left out of something everyone else could participate in.

About ten minutes after the movie started, the person got up and left, but then returned, sitting one seat away from me. We watched the action together. I glanced at them a few times, heard laugher, smooth and easy—not hard or loud or arrogant like some laughs can be. As the film ended, the person leaned over and handed me a note. It said they come there every Monday, Friday, and Saturday. It said their name was Elijah and their pronouns were they/them. They wrote: *next time, perhaps the movie ends happily???* Their script was tight and small but very legible. The three question marks made me smile.

I went again the next day.

I didn't admit to myself that I was considering it until the afternoon rolled around and I stood looking at my outfit in the mirror.

It happened simply enough. I sat in the back corner, and they showed up about ten minutes into the film. They looked at me, and in the dark I saw their eyes wide and excited. The pale skin along their neck illuminated by the light on the screen. They had to be over six feet, so they slid low into the seat.

A couple sat about ten rows down from us, munching on popcorn. They whispered, Are you ok with this?

Yes, I whispered.

They reached over and rubbed my dick through my pants. They slowly got me hard and then unzipped me and began jacking me off so slowly—so slowly I didn't think I would even come. I didn't help them one bit. It felt almost juvenile: in the dark, no kissing, clothes on. They even pinched the skin on my cock with the zipper's teeth. I didn't say anything. They didn't say anything. But it worked—this quiet, delicate build up, until I leaned my head back and felt myself coming. I looked down at my cock and their fingers, the wrinkled knuckles, the opaqueness of nails in the theater light. Then I asked if they wanted me to do something for them. They nodded, and I reached over. Their cock was already out and hard and slick with precum. I wanted it in my mouth, but it seemed too awkward in the cramped space, so I licked my palms and gripped their cock, slender and long. It took only a minute. There was something tender about the way they came without making a sound, thighs flexing, belly sucking in. A quiet reverence. It was almost spiritual. They wiped us both up with what looked like a cloth diaper. They then left, tapping my thigh a few times like they were saying goodbye.

I felt wonderful until the following Monday, when I walked into the lobby of the theater and saw them standing behind the concession counter with two coworkers. I recognized them immediately. The thin body, the long neck, the doughy face, the acne, the towel that hung from their belt—the same they used to clean us up—the corporate, usher attire.

How had I not realized they worked at the movie theater and weren't a customer like me? They grinned conspiratorially. I felt nauseous.

They said, Hello, sir. May I serve you? They chuckled like something was funny.

I frowned as I glanced at the coworkers. All of them looked like college students. I hadn't realized they were so young. I bought popcorn and went into the theater. When they sat next to me, they whispered, I can't stay right now, but if you're free tomorrow...

I wanted to yell at them. I felt tricked. It bothered me too that they seemed so fucking happy. In the dark of the theater it had been so easy, but now it wasn't. I was angry because the more you knew, the more complicated things were.

With Sandra Bullock's face on the screen, I said, You should have ignored me out there. I'm sorry, but this can't happen again.

They said, Why are you making things weird? You're right. This won't happen again.

I waited through the entire movie, and when I walked through the lobby, not a single one of them looked my way.

Tonight I'm sitting at The Avenue, the last real dive bar in Temescal, with faded and crooked framed Budweiser posters and Christmas lights strung up by tacks, only these lights never come down. These are like college dorm-room lights. First apartment lights. They even blink on and off.

I'm wondering what the chances are of ever being intimate with someone without complications, without knowledge, familiarity, getting in the way.

Jason's trying to cheer me up. I told him the story of breaking up with Jared and Stella's pregnancy and my failed attempts at dating and even the movie theater rejection. I appreciate that he hasn't tried to offer any advice. He just said, I'm taking you out. He promised to be my wingperson.

He's invited two of his friends, Dolly and Trevor, and as the evening draws out, I start thinking my recent dating luck might change with either or both of them.

We all agree eggnog is fucking disgusting.

Dolly, thin and androgynous, hair pulled back tightly in a bun, makes gagging sounds that strangely excite me. Trevor, some mixed-race young man, has his hair pulled back in an identical bun—the only difference being that his is covered by an orange beanie, giving it the look of the reservoir tip of a condom. He tosses out adjectives like *frothy, creamy*, and *spicy,* words that should never be used to describe a cold beverage. Even Jason can't stand the stuff, though he argues that if you put enough bourbon in it, the aftertaste is similar to Dr. Pepper. We give him so much shit, he almost orders a round for us, but the bartender informs Jason that he too hates eggnog and would never serve it.

Jason yells, Man, you got to try new things. You never know when you'll get lucky!

We're debating what's the worst thing about the holiday season, and Trevor shares a tidbit about how SantaCon used to be an anarchist thing to fuck with consumers, and now it's some bro-party. He spits out *bro* like phlegm. We banter about how Christianity consumed pagan rituals that taught respect for each other and the earth, how consumerist practices divorce us from our humanity, how Thanksgiving makes us think of genocide, how irritating chorales are. I share the story of reading "The Night Before Christmas" so many damn times to my daughter that I vowed never to utter the clichéd last line ever again. I pause for drama, hoping someone will blurt out the line, but no one does—or maybe they're waiting to see if I will break my promise.

We all sit in silence. I stare at Dolly's red lips and chipped front tooth, Jason's greasy blond hair, Trevor's bright orange beanie and slightly crooked nose.

You all know it, I demand.

All three pretend never to have heard *Merry Christmas to all, and to all a good night.*

Trevor breaks the stalemate by saying, The only good thing is mistletoe.

Dolly sips her IPA and says, What's good about a holiday invention that perpetuates patriarchal hegemony? If you walk under it, you have to kiss someone. What does that teach kids about consent?

I want to argue, but I realize she's totally right. I immediately want to Google the origin of mistletoe, believing something must be redeemable about the tradition, but we've stacked our phones on the table, and the person who touches theirs first has to buy all our drinks.

Jason saves us from the silence that goes on a beat too long by bringing up the one other thing we all can agree on besides hating eggnog: loving resolutions. Beginning anew. Recommitments.

Jason says, I want to be less judgmental. More kind. More trusting. Like maybe SantaCon ain't that bad.

Trevor adds, I want hotter sex, which means perhaps being more discerning. I also guess I want to try eggnog with bourbon.

Trevor and Jason actually bump fists.

Dolly says, I want to get lucky. In all the ways.

They look at me. I imagine saying: *I want to be more fearless, to trust my heart, to love my body. I want to dance more, cook more, invite people over to my apartment more. I want to actually ask someone out on a date rather than meeting them online. I want to feel connected.* But I say simply, I want to try harder.

Dolly asks, At what?

I say, At all the things, thinking I'm clever. I wink as well.

When we decide to leave, Jason and Trevor go to the bar both to pay and to plead for the bartender to order some eggnog before the holiday season ends. Dolly and I head to the bathroom, but both doors are locked, so we stand on opposite sides of the hall facing each other.

It was nice to meet you, I say.

It was, she says.

I want to ask her out, but I don't. I fight the urge to take out my phone. Trying not to stare at her smirking mouth, her chipped front tooth, I look down and see the skin of her ankles.

She laughs and says, Look up.

We are standing under a big bunch of mistletoe. Someone has written in sharpie on the ceiling above it: *Don't be afraid!*

Suddenly I feel her pull me in for a kiss. Right before she places her lips on mine, she whispers, You ok with this?

I nod.

She says, I need a *Yes, Dolly*.

I say, Yes, Dolly.

She sucks my bottom lip into her mouth and bites down hard.

I hear Trevor ask, And are you ok with this?

I say, Yes, Dolly, even though I know it's Trevor, but I'm not thinking at all with my brain.

I feel his hands slip down my thighs. His tongue licks my neck. I pull away to look at him, but he and Dolly start to kiss, still holding my body tight against theirs. I don't have time to appreciate it because both bathroom doors open, and we pull apart to let the emerging people pass.

Dolly motions me into one of the open bathrooms, then yanks Trevor into the other one with her.

I stand at the urinal under horrific lighting: a bluish-hued fluorescent bulb in a red bathroom. I look sickly green. I take out my cock and hold it lovingly. It's that perfect cock fullness, not completely erect but thick and on the verge. I close my eyes and switch hands holding my cock, left, right, left, but stop because I'm turning myself on and it becomes difficult to pee. I try to listen to what's happening in the next room, but I can't hear anything. I breathe in and out and my cock softens and I feel myself pee.

When I step out, the other door is open, and Trevor and Dolly are nowhere in sight.

I find them with Jason out in front of the bar, gathered around bikes locked together. One by one, they free the bikes from each other. It feels like ceremony. Like ritual. My lips still zing from Dolly's teeth.

She gets on her bike and turns to us and says in her biggest holiday voice, Merry Christmas to all and to all a hella lucky night.

Trevor hugs Jason and says, Good to see you again. Then he looks at me and says, I'd invite you back to my place, but I have family visiting. Maybe next time?

I nod.

Good. I work at the bookstore in downtown Oakland. Stop by, he says and bikes away with Dolly.

Jason and I stand outside in silence for a minute. It's cold but dry. We are both biking to the same neighborhood, but I don't know exactly where he lives. I almost ask but realize that might come off awkwardly.

Want to have a nightcap at Nicks? I ask.

That could be nice. And sorry about that. They can be a bit intense.

No more intense than you, my friend.

All right JG, bring it on. Let's get real. You think I'm intense? I can see he's smiling.

Yes. I grin.

And you mean this in a good way, right?

I mean this in a beautiful way.

Then thank you. That's my resolution. Say *thank you* more often.

We bike ride down Shattuck, and I admire all the houses with Christmas lights, then wonder about those houses without them. Do they not have kids, and what do single people living by themselves do to get in the festive spirit? When we get to Nicks, there is some company Christmas party spilling out the door. The door guy is yelling at people to get back inside. He's clapping his hand against his paperback book, but everyone just ignores him.

Not interested, Jason says.

Me either. See you later, I say.

Tell me if you stop by the bookstore, Jason says and peddles away.

11

King Pleasure

I think I'm depressed. Maybe I need to stop dating, focus on self-care. I start with my daily routine. In the morning I shave and trim my mustache and eyebrows. I pat my belly and look at it from both sides. I shower. I dry off. I look at my pubic hair. I like it trimmed tight and neat, and I like my balls smooth, but I hate to shave there, so I cut the hairs right to the skin using long silver scissors—pulling scrotum skin with one hand and holding scissors with the other. It's a delicate and dangerous operation. I find it relaxing.

I end my routine by holding my penis. I think of where it's been. I think of it inside, actually inside, another person's body, a body much like mine. The asses and pussies and mouths. The tenderness of orifices. It almost excites me. I don't masturbate or fantasize, though. I just hold it and close my eyes and feel the blood pulse, pulse. The beat of blood reminds me I'm alive.

I concentrate on my work, but that's just work. The usual answering of emails, sending mockups and quotes. I sometimes review Python or Java to learn more about the backend of websites. Generally, though, I create the frontends, what viewers experience, using HTML or CSS. It's simply repetition and review. There is no desire other than the paycheck, necessity. Usually I distract myself by thinking about Jared, but now I have trouble doing that. I still have *seeing someone* as my status on my social media, and so does he. I check. And when I see that he hasn't changed it, I feel thankful and still loved. Like he still believes in us, even though he put the proverbial ball in my court, and I did nothing. I let the opportunity pass. He barely reaches out anymore, but that makes sense. I come with a lot of shit. He wanted a relationship. I wanted safety. Clearly, an impasse. Relationships are never safe or easy or calm. They are risky. Fraught. They aren't guaranteed.

I saw him a week ago out in front of a restaurant that we'd never been to with another person. They seemed casual, but the way Jared stood next to them with his legs open and welcoming, I knew they were lovers.

I just biked by and went home.

I think about my daughter, pregnant, five hundred miles away.

I think about the purpose of loneliness. In my free time, which I now have way too much of, I bike around—not for exercise as I did initially. Now I do it to feel connected.

I usually bike to Berkeley High around 3:45, when school ends and teenagers brazenly take over the sidewalks and roads as they make their way off campus. I zip between students who remind me of my daughter. I look at the angry faces of drivers stuck in their cars as swaths of teens refuse to let them through the crosswalks. I enjoy the thrill of biking along congested streets of Berkeley and Oakland. I bike along the commerce of Telegraph Avenue and the privilege of College Avenue and the diversity of Shattuck. I bike Grizzly Peak when I feel like sweating. I bike around Lake Merritt to see little kids and parents together or clusters of hipsters drinking beer from cans.

I get coffee at the various cafés around my apartment. I bring no work and no reading, so it's just me and coffee and awkward nothingness while everyone has a phone or laptop or book in front of them.

I look for eye contact.

I don't get any, until Janet.

She's wrapped in a scarf that makes her head seem way too small. The scarf, red and black, balances on her shoulders like it was squeezed from a tube of toothpaste. It's definitely brisk out, but the huge scarf seems a bit much. She appears to be in her early thirties, a welcome reprieve from the deluge of twenty-year-olds in the coffee shop.

As she sits across from me at the communal table, she has nothing in front of her except a donut and a cup of tea, the string with the paper tab dangling down.

I am halfway through my double Americano and a lemon bar.

We inadvertently fall into a pattern. When she sips, I sip. When she takes a bite, I take a bite.

She smiles and says, Don't copy me.

I say, I started first.

She says, Ok, I'll change it up.

Next time, as I sip, she takes a bite. Despite her trying to create a different rhythm, we match up again a few minutes later.

I laugh a little and blow the powdered sugar off the top of my lemon bar. She grins and proceeds to wind the string with the paper tab around the handle of her mug. She has a round pleasant freckly face and is not at all my type. I think of the women I've been attracted to. Betsy was an anomaly. Short and stocky. Betsy I loved because I was a boy when I met her, and she loved me like I was a man. The women that followed her were more like the boy I was: thin, pliable, defensively arrogant, and slightly skittish.

This woman is too confident. She has this black curly hair that's shaved around the sides, with a mop of black ringlets bouncing about the top her head. She also has grandmother cat-eye glasses. But her smile is relaxing, so even though I am not interested, I return it, then quickly look away. I don't want to be that guy, even though I feel like that guy at this coffee shop where everyone is so young. I haven't been sleeping well lately. Maybe I'm just in a bad mood and it's affecting everything. I'm thinking about getting up and going outside when she speaks to me.

You biked here, right?

I did, I say.

I like that you bike, she comments.

I bike a lot, I say.

I like that, a lot, she says, then continues, I'm meeting my boyfriend in a few minutes. But we should hang out. We should bike.

With your boyfriend? I ask.

No. You and me, she says. I'm Janet. I just moved here, and I'm looking to meet some new people.

She slides me her number and straps on her helmet, one of those very round motorcycle kind, with stickers affixed to the gray plastic: *share the road, clitoral mass, one less fixie.*

I don't call her. I can't bring myself to call her. I can't accept that I'm that lonely. But I do return to the coffee shop repeatedly.

I see her a week later. I am outside drinking an Americano, and she bikes past me. She waves and then circles back and rides up, unclipping her helmet. It's one of those glorious early spring days, chilly yet bright, and she's wearing a t-shirt with the sleeves cut out and yoga pants. You can see the color of her bra: mauve with black lace.

She says, Hi. Are you free for the next couple hours?

In the past I'd say, *Free till five, when my daughter comes home* or *when Jared gets off work.* Using Stella as an excuse still feels instinctual. Using Jared still feels hopeful. Like I still have places I need to be, even though I don't.

I look at her flushed face, a couple zits scabbed over on her chin. I wonder if she breaks out when she menstruates like my daughter does.

I say, Yes. I'm free, a bit too eagerly.

Come with me. There's this Basquiat show I want to check out at the Oakland Museum.

Janet and I bike along the sanctioned Bike Boulevards, taking up the full lane. It's late afternoon, but it feels like the sun will never go down, the light bright and illuminating everything.

I just listen while she tells me about graduating from a Chinese medicine school, learning acupuncture, and taking a few months off to relax before setting up her practice.

You practice on yourself first, she says. You practice diagnosing yourself and then your classmates. It's a hoot. That was the best part, looking at people's bodies, smelling them, questioning them. You even ask about their poop.

She says this like it would be a great thing to do at a party.

I imagine the possibilities of reading the body like a medical book. I imagine those Chinese medicine charts with numbers and lines and diagrams sweeping across the body connecting one thing to another thing, individual points creating a whole.

I ask, Do you know how to help someone sleep?

She says, You?

I say, Lately I've had a hard time staying asleep once I fall asleep.

She lets go of her handlebars to look back at me. She says, I can treat you if you want. I help my boyfriend all the time.

Once we get to the museum, we have less than an hour before closing. The place is empty. We have room after room to ourselves. I walk up to a Mel Ramos painting, a woman leaning on a car, the colors vibrant and glowing. I lean in and see the way the brush strokes make up her skin. I lean back to find the moment the brush strokes become indiscernible. The moment the illusion of skin becomes real.

Juan! Hey, Juan! Here it is, Janet calls.

I follow the sound and enter a dim room to see her standing, hands on hips, in front of a number of paintings. They've been placed in a room by themselves, with a bench in the middle to encourage contemplation and comfort. We start with the smaller ones: stick bodies, wild hair, and scribbly hands with three fingers like claws. The colors bold. The lines frenetic, almost childish, but determined. The thing that strikes me is how the scribbles and lines are like the medical charts I imagine Janet studied. They appear like compass markings. Like legends on maps. Like if I looked past the lines and swirls and paint and color I'd find something important.

The biggest painting, *King Pleasure*, is soothing, almost boring after the others. It's mostly empty space that's a rich mustard-yellow, Basquiat's trademark crown drawn with plain ragged lines right in the center of the picture. He's filled it in with a dull brown. There's a small sword off to the side of the crown, but he's scribbled over it. There's three other things circling the crown, but he's completely scribbled over them. Completely. You can't know what was there. You will never know. Finally, the words *King Pleasure* are written out and underlined, with the final *e* scribbled out as well. The emptiness of the canvas makes me uncomfortable. It feels arrogant or tragic.

Janet says, I love the way something so simple can mean so much.

I say, It does seem so simple. But what does it mean?

She says, It means . . . well, I like to think it means you are your own pleasure.

I like that, I say.

We stand in silence for a minute.

She says, Stick out your tongue, and let's see what it says.

I face her. I feel self-conscious about my breath, about the color of my tongue.

She cups my chin firmly but with care. She tilts my head to the light.

I stick out my tongue and she leans in.

She says, I would scrape the coating on your tongue. Curdy tongue, it's called. It can tell you a lot about a person's health, but I haven't washed my hands.

It's ok, I say quickly, not wanting her to stop.

She doesn't hesitate. She touches my tongue, slides a finger across it. She looks at it and smells it, her face expressionless, clinical.

She does it again, and this time she leaves her finger on my tongue for a second, about to scrape it—but before she does, I close my mouth around her finger and hold it there.

She laughs but doesn't pull her finger out.

I keep my mouth closed and shut my eyes. I imagine taking her entire hand into my mouth, her pleasant round freckly face into my mouth. I imagine other things: my daughter, the empty space on the canvas, Jared's thighs and mouth and cock. I imagine placing all the things I care about, all the things I love, into my mouth. I imagine how full I would feel, how happy, how like a king.

12

How to Mend Broken Things

It's been over a week since I've seen Jason, his greasy face and earnest energy, and without him the bar seems dull, the carpet more nasty. In his absence I realize I have sat next to his crusty ass weekly for over four years. He's like my longest relationship going besides Betsy, besides Stella. He's my only success. Since my love life and my family life have fallen apart, Jason's absence stands out even more. I can't lose him too.

I'll see him biking at times during the week, his black pants cut and sewn to the midcalf, his front basket an old milk crate and his bike frame covered in stickers. He lives only a few blocks down from me, but I still don't know exactly where. When we do run into each other, we stop and chat about some event or issue. Jason always with his politics. Once I teased him about his white boy guilt.

He said, Just because you're Mexican...

Chicano, I corrected, remembering the lecture my father used to give me about how I wouldn't survive a day in Mexico around real Mexicans.

Not to correct you, but I think it's Chicanx now.

See, you feeling guilty right now, I said.

He smiled and continued, As I was saying before being interrupted. Just because you're a POC doesn't mean you're political by default. It takes work to stay conscious of what's happening in the world and how you affect it.

You think we can affect anything?

Of course, he answered with a seriousness that impressed me.

When he's not there a third night, I wonder how much I actually know about him. Strange that I've shared countless beers with him, debated sports and politics, introduced him to my lover, sung karaoke with him—even hung out with him and his own crew of friends, Dolly and Trevor, at that other bar—but I can't remember any significant information about his life.

There's a way men can talk and never say a thing.

I call Bob over. Have you seen Jason lately? I ask.

He pauses, hands flat out on the bar as he stands there thinking. I haven't.

What does he do? I ask. You know, to make that cheddar.

Bob knows I'm joking, but he grimaces and splashes more sparkly water in my glass.

You know, I never asked, he says.

When Jason's at the bar, he's entertaining without being aggressive. He's too grimy to be vain. He just kind of makes me feel welcome to be myself. I needed that.

The last time we were at Nicks together, the Forty-Niners were embroiled in some off-field drama about a player's arrest. The highlights were silently playing as Jason commented on how badly the organization was handling the situation—speaking louder than usual to be heard over someone's horrible attempt at a Tom Waits song.

Why are you so happy? I asked, pretending ignorance. Are you a Raiders fan?

From somewhere behind me came the classic *Raaaaiders* chant, yelled anytime someone caught wind of the word.

On cue, Jason yelled back, like a straight male homing beacon.

He said, It's true, I am a Raider fan, but that's not why I'm smiling. He paused

I took the bait. Ok, so why are you smiling?

He shifted in his chair to face me. He said, When you're in a position that what you do or say has real social impact, and you say homophobic shit like those guys on the 'Niners did, it's just insane. It's inexcusable. It breaks something. You can't root for them.

What would you do if you were there when they said it? I asked.

He shook his head. I have no idea, but when the time comes to say something important, I hope I'll have the courage to do so.

Later that evening, the third without Jason seated next to me, I ask Frankie and Susan if they've seen him. Nobody has.

The next morning I make my coffee and sit down to work, but it's hard to focus. I wonder what Jared's doing, if he's seeing someone else yet. I wonder what my daughter's doing, how she and her boyfriend are faring. I even wonder about the baby.

When I finally take a break, I grab my bike and walk it outside, but instead of getting on it, I push it down the sidewalk. I walk up the street—one block, two—looking on both sides for his bike. Finally I see it four blocks down on the opposite side, locked to a railing on the second floor of an apartment building. Its front rim is bent like it has been in an accident.

I stand for a few minutes, not sure what to do. Finally, I lock my bike and climb the steps to the stoop, crowded with three bowls of cat food and about ten pots of various succulents. I recognize a few. Beans and rice my mother called the one I see in a blue pot. Aloe vera, of course. But there're some crazy-looking ones as well.

I knock. Nothing. I knock again and shout, Jason, Jason, it's me, Juan.

The door swings open, and Jason is standing there shirtless, in pinstriped boxers, with an arm in a sling and bandages on his shoulder and face. His chest sports what look like homemade tattoos of geometrical shapes and the letters *FTP*.

We don't say anything, but he moves to let me in.

The place is dirty, stacked pizza boxes, Chinese-food containers, empty bottles of coconut water. I can see right into the kitchen. There's a sink full of dishes.

Fuck, I say. What the hell happened?

He tells me about being doored, about thinking he was going to die, about looking up at this young woman's face, the way she smiled, the way she said *It looks worse than it really is*, the way he knew she was lying because she kept patting his arm in that disingenuous way.

He says, She sat there with me while I waited for the ambulance. She kept smiling and asking me questions like she was keeping my mind off the fact that my arm was dangling like a wet noodle.

Oh, stop, I say.

She says to me, *Do you think the universe is telling you to slow down?*

He laughs at this, a big round laugh that is full of anger and frustration and pain.

What did you say? I ask.

I said it didn't have to tell me this emphatically.

You were able to use the word emphatically?

He says, I broke my arm, not my vocabulary.

He doesn't smile like I want him to. He says, I felt like shit the first few days after.

You broke your arm. You're supposed to feel like shit, I say.

I know, but it was more emotional for some reason. I felt depressed. I kept wanting to hug that woman who kept telling me it was going to be ok, who kept that fake smile on her face. I realized I never even got her name. I never thanked her.

I hear in his voice that he's trying to hide his pain. His breath is going in and out in shaky waves.

I want to say something, but I just keep nodding. He keeps breathing. He closes his eyes and leans back on the couch. I watch him for a few minutes. I realize he's falling asleep. I stand and walk to the kitchen. For the next hour, I do the dishes, empty the trash, sweep the floor.

I hear him call, Ugly Kitty.

When I look over, there are three cats—one really mangy with half an ear gone, the two others cleaner and prettier.

I say, I never knew you were a cat dude.

He says, I'm not really, but they like me. They like my house. I was told by a close friend that it's good luck when a cat adopts your house.

I say, Maybe it's because you put that food in front of your door.

He tells me their names are Ugly Kitty (the one with the messed up ear), Fluffy Kitty (a big fluffy cat), and Orange Kitty (who is in fact orange).

I say, You put a lot of thought into the names, I can tell, and what's up with those plants?

The carnivorous ones? he says.

They're carnivorous?

A few of them are. See, I'm not just a cat dude. The flies that the cat food attracts are what feeds the plants. It's a system, a system of things that help each other. Symbiotic.

Neither of us says anything for a minute.

Can I make you dinner?

I see him hesitate.

I say, My mother taught me that when someone offers to do something nice for you, simply say *yes* and *thank you*.

It sounds so easy, he says. Yes. And thank you.

You're welcome, I say.

After a dinner of noodles with red sauce and a salad, we sit on the couch, and Jason offers me a Percocet. I've never tried one, but I accept. I tell him about how Stella teased me about always cooking pasta with red sauce. We play dominos for an hour, until he gets sleepy. My body feels light, weightless from the pill. Ugly Kitty gets up on his lap and treats it like a pillow. The other ones sit next to him, purring.

How'd Ugly Kitty get ugly?

Don't know. He showed up, and I nursed him back. He was the first one.

I ask, Are you dating someone?

He shifts on the couch, trying to get more comfortable. Her name's Rosa. She's a long-time lover, he says. Like it's a title. Like the implications of it are universal, obvious.

Long-time lover. I like that, I say.

He says, We love each other. That's what counts.

Where is she? I ask, worried that maybe he hasn't told her what happened to him yet.

She's traveling right now. She'll be back soon.

Does she know? I ask.

I'll tell her. I don't want her to stress.

I nod, considering what we say and don't say to each other because we worry. Because we are embarrassed, scared, hurt. I want to say something meaningful.

I say, You are going to get better, you know.

He says, I know. I just forgot how much work it takes to mend.

You've got help, I say, and reach out to cup his good shoulder.

How are you and Jared? Are you seeing each other again? Is it repairable?

I shake my head.

I'm your friend, he says. I'm on your side. I don't know what happened. But let me tell you something. I think you should work it out. You were so much calmer, more relaxed, when you were seeing him.

I just shrug.

I'm not trying to be mean—let's just blame it on the Percocet— but you can't keep everything all bottled up. You've got to go for what makes you happy.

Happy? I ask. What does that even mean?

I know what it sounds like, but trust me. Discover what makes your heart race.

What does that to you? I ask to get the subject off of me and my racing heart. He closes his eyes and sinks back into his couch cushions.

He says, I fucking love Ugly Kitty and those plants outside. It makes me so happy to see them when I come home. And music. God, I love music. And stories about people who do the right thing in face of so many reasons not to. And Rosa. Yummy Rosa. And Nicks. And you.

He sits up quickly and looks hard at me, saying, Thank you for coming over. For finding me.

You're welcome, I say awkwardly.

And these goddamn drugs. They're pure joy. They make my heart race.

I move to get up, thinking it's time to go, but he catches my arm.

He says, All that is to say that Jared clearly made you happy. Whatever you thought wasn't working, or that you couldn't give or compromise on, you should reconsider.

Why do you think it was my doing? I say, feeling defensive.

Juan, I love you and all, but you are a seriously closed fist. Patriarchy's a fucker. Messes men up. He smiles and continues, Me too, if I'm being truthful.

I want to leave, but I have to ask: What do you do to pay the rent? What's your real job?

He says, What's with all your questions?

I say, I realized I never asked you.

Landscaping, tiling, basic home-repair stuff. But lately I've been modeling for art students at Cal. He grins, and his bandage stretches his skin across his cheek. It looks painful, but I laugh.

He says, I'm serious. Have you seen my thighs?

I have, I say.

He lifts his legs up and reclines on the sofa. He looks exhausted, lying there covered in cats.

I let myself out and head back toward my house, but instead of stopping, I bike past, all the way up to Nicks.

I say to Bob, Jason has a long-time lover. Her name's Rosa. She's traveling now. He just broke his arm in a bike accident, so that's why he hasn't been here. In case you were wondering.

Bob stares intently at me as I relay all the information.

Then he says, What day is it? You're not usually here today, right?

It makes me feel good that he knows this about me.

I say, He's also a model. That's what he does for money. He models for art students.

Naked? Bob laughs. Jason? Really?

That's what he said, I say. I just think it's important that we know things about each other.

Fair enough. And that does make sense, Bob says. That dude's always talking about his damn biker thighs.

13

Lost Causes

It's four in the morning, and my phone rings. First my landline. I ignore it. No one I want to speak to calls me on that line anymore. Then my cell phone. I ignore it too, because it's four in the morning. But then my landline rings again. At that point, I think of my Stella and Byron and the baby and quickly reach out to grab the receiver. I realize it's now a strange sensation to answer a call not knowing who it might be.

Ah, Juanito. It's your mother. I'm calling about your father, she says and leaves that word hanging out there.

My father, I repeat.

Yes, your father, and again she leaves the word dangling, as though it has meaning, as though it's sacred—but all I picture is an orange jumpsuit. A bushy mustache. A dirty look.

Neither of us says a thing.

Finally, she breathes in deeply. I imagine her mouth with the deep red lipstick, but it's four in the morning, so she certainly isn't wearing it now. I feel my heart beat faster and taste the staleness of my mouth.

Juan, she says, he died.

My mind blanks. When? I ask automatically.

At seven in the morning yesterday. The prison will tell us when to claim the body. He wanted to be cremated, so I can handle that, if you want. But there's his stuff. He has boxes in my garage. You should come down and go through them.

Yes, I say.

He went peacefully, they said. Died in his bunk. Just all that bad living, I think. All his bad choices catching up to him.

After another pause, she continues, I love you. You're in my prayers. You always are.

I feel like she's trying to tell me something about my bad choices. I say, Thank you. I hear her breathing through the phone. Alive. I imagine her in the living room of her house in Salinas, surrounded by her little porcelain statuettes. I imagine her head shaking to the left, to the right, to the left, repeatedly and slowly.

Mama, I whisper. Are you ok?

It takes her a moment to respond. Such a waste, Mijo. Such a waste.

In the early morning darkness, I wait for her to continue.

He was so much more than the man you knew. So different. So loving.

I remember the last time he touched me. My graduation. He still lived at our house in San Jose, but he was never there. I recall the way my heart beat faster whenever I heard his Chevy Nova rumbling down the street. He showed up one morning. Opened my bedroom door. I could tell he'd been up a while. I assumed all night, from the way he smelled. Stale beer. Acrid cigarette smoke. I kept my eyes closed. He stood above me. He reached down and put his hand on my head, softly, trying not to wake me. He turned and left the room. I heard him yell at my mother, asking why she let me keep my room like a pigsty.

What happened to him? I ask her now.

I don't know. Whatever happens to all our men. They give up. I love you. Call me later.

Again I say, Thank you.

I hang up. I am not sure why I thanked her. I rise and sit on the edge of the bed. I think about church and my father's refusal to go when my mother begged him to. I remember her telling him they would pray for him. My father would laugh. He'd say, It won't help, and slap my shoulder like we were in it together.

The last real conversation I had with him ended with his laughter. He possessed a good laugh. Filled a room. Made everyone around him smile and look to see what was so funny.

I woke one morning to find him on the couch in Levis and a white tank top. He had no socks on, and he was clipping his toe nails. The skin of his feet so much lighter than his arms and shoulders and neck.

Juanito, can you fill my coffee?

I grabbed his cup, and when I returned to him, he had his arm stretched across the couch and a neat pile of nail clippings on the coffee table in front of him.

Sit.

I sat.

He sipped the coffee and seemed to relax into the sofa with me next to him.

You still seeing the white girl? What's her name?

Betsy. Yeah, we still hang out.

He grinned and nodded. He said, I was worried about you.

I knew what he alluded to, but I couldn't say anything to him. I wouldn't. There was nothing to be gained. And I was afraid.

So how's the other stuff going?

Stuff?

You know. Don't act stupid. School, and you got a job right? At ...

Radio Shack. Yes. School's almost done.

I know what month it is. You set up your dorm situation at the university?

Me and a couple friends were thinking about moving to Oakland. It's cheaper, and I can transfer my job up there too.

The ghetto? Why you want to move around them. You going to get jumped.

I just looked at him.

Because you're not black. He started to laugh.

I can take care of myself.

His laughing escalated. Like that was the funniest thing he'd heard in a while. He hugged me and said, Yeah, right, my little vato. You can fuck people up. You won't take no shit. He stood up and finished his coffee and sang some song on his way to his room.

I hate memories. I know I won't go back to sleep, so I get up and shower. Afterward I stand in the middle of the room and drop the towel to the floor. I stand there wrapped in the darkness, the quiet. I start dressing in my biking clothes. I hustle to the door with my bike and head north. I fly down King and turn up Spruce as the hills to the east take shape out of the darkness, the sky purples and oranges.

I stop about a hundred yards from Indian Rock, a massive rock outcropping in the middle of million-dollar homes in North Berkeley. Kids come to get stoned and watch the sunset, and rock climbers come to practice bouldering. I wonder if they need belay partners to do that. I walk my bike to the base and drop it against some shrubs lining the park. I realize I don't even have my lock with me. I climb the rocks to the top and watch the city lights of Oakland and San Francisco dim, watch the Bay Bridge transform from the sparkling clarity of white and red lights to the drab gray seriousness of the morning commute.

I bike home as fast as I can, and when I get to my street, I ride past my house. I haul my bike up to Jason's apartment and knock. There is the stillness of people sleeping. I guess it's at least seven or seven thirty. I don't let it stop me. I knock again, harder.

He opens the door and then his mouth, as if he is about to say something about the time and whether I am crazy. But something makes him stop. The skin on his cheek just under his eye is a mottled pale pink from the accident.

Wow. Looks like the scab fell off, I say.

He waits a second and says, I picked it off. I couldn't help it.

It's been two weeks since I discovered he broke his arm. He still hasn't come out to the bar. I've stopped by a few times to bring beer, play a game of dominos, and just make sure he's feeling all right.

He opens the door wider, says, You're lucky I get up this early. What would you have done if I was sleeping?

I don't know how to answer. I stare at him as he walks to the kitchen. I glance at the couch, at some pink-and-brown crocheted Afghan that looks like it was made by a grandmother. I see his three cats. I feel like they're watching me.

He says, It doesn't matter. I'm up, and I'm watching bad '90s alt rock videos on the computer.

Sounds fun, I say.

He doesn't ask why I'm here. He simply gets a mug and pours some coffee from his coffee maker. No cream or sugar. The mug is really hard to hold because it has this handle that is in the shape of a cow.

He sits on the couch and motions me to join him, then grimaces like the movement hurt his wrist.

I say, I met this woman named Janet who's an acupuncturist. She told me about some herbs to help me sleep. You should maybe see her for your arm.

Give me her number. Is this woman a lover? He drags out the word *lover*.

No. Just a friend. But she's cool, and she's into all that healthy herbal stuff.

Nice, he says. He sips his coffee as if he's waiting for something else to happen. Then he says, Remember this? and clicks the space bar.

The video for Papa Roach's *Last Resort* comes on his computer screen.

I smile immediately. I nod to the beat, and he does too. I can't help it. I start singing: *Cut my life into pieces. I've reached my last resort.*

He joins in, and together we sing the rest.

When it's over, I say, That's actually a pretty good song.

No shit, he says.

We cycle through more songs, so many I feel like we are watching a VH1 musical history show: P.O.D, Stone Temple Pilots, System of a Down, Nine Inch Nails. We take turns standing and singing, gesticulating for effect. It's shocking how many bad songs we know by heart. At one point he's singing a horrifically catchy one by Sigur Rós, and he suddenly stops and asks, So why'd you come over this morning, Juan?

I say nothing for a minute.

He says, I know it's bad news. You look upset.

I am, I say, I should probably take something.

Are you sick?

I shake my head. I say, My father died.

He just looks at me.

He says, Let me grab the Percocet.

I look at my fingers gingerly holding the cow coffee mug.

What are you going to do? he asks.

I need to drive to Salinas. I'll go tomorrow, I guess. Spend some time there.

Good, he says. That gives us time to get a goodbye drink tonight at the bar.

No way. It's Saturday, I say.

Believe me, when a parent dies, you can go anytime you fucking want.

Thanks, I say.

Were you close? he asks.

No, I say. My father was a dick.

Did you get a chance to tell him that? he asks.

I didn't.

That sucks. But it's never too late. Tell me why your dad was a dick.

I say, When I was sixteen, he found me sitting with a friend in high school. Mike Johnson. We had never even touched each other in a sexual way. My father was short and stocky. He walked in the room, saw me looking at a magazine Mike was holding. He paused and then walked over. I smiled at him and said, *Hello*. He looked at me and then looked at Mike. He said to us, *Look at you two all snuggled up like a couple of faggots. I'd be careful.* He turned and left.

What happened after that? Jason asks.

Mike never came over again. I started to leave my neighborhood as much as I could. Took classes at a college across town, in one of those programs helping Chicano students get into UCs, and then I met Betsy.

Well, it's true. Your dad was a dick.

I stare blankly at the computer, the screensaver a pulsing triangle morphing into a rectangle then into a circle repeatedly.

I say, When my father was arrested after I moved to Oakland, I felt relief. After he was arrested, my mother moved back to her hometown. I ran. She ran. He must've realized this, how hated he was. He never once reached out to me or my mother, not during the trial or after he was sentenced.

Don't answer this if it's not my business, but what was he arrested for?

No, it's not a problem. Little things that added up, and then he got into some brawl and put someone in the hospital. That was the third strike. He was out.

Fucking racist policing, man. I'm sorry.

I shrug.

He pats my knee and gets up to get more coffee.

I don't know what's worse. Your dad and his homophobic bullshit or my dad and how he constantly tried to be just one of the boys.

My dad was worse, I say flatly.

He looks at me and says, True. You're right. But seriously, let me tell you, my dad literally wanted to do everything with us. Like we lived in Walnut Creek, and he offered to drive us to shows at Gilman Street, but he wanted to come to the show too.

I've been to Walnut Creek. Took Stella to the big shopping mall. No other reason to go to Walnut Creek.

Stella's been to that punk club, but I haven't.

And you shouldn't. Not if your daughter is there. Because you're her father. But my father would be like, *Isn't it an all-ages club?* And we'd say, *Yes.* And he said, *Well, why do they discriminate against a fifty-year-old fiscally conservative yet socially liberal guy like me.* And then he'd laugh. He had the most cartoonish laugh. *Yuckyuck-yuck.*

The way Jason uses voices and stands up while he narrates makes me relax back into the sofa. I pet Ugly Kitty and laugh.

It feels good to laugh.

When I get to my apartment, I pace around the living room. I make eggs. Perfectly scrambled. I remember some stupid fight with Jared about runny eggs and how I refused to eat them. I remember all the pointless arguments with Stella, with Betsy. I think of all the arguments I wish I'd had with my father.

I call Betsy.

Hello Juan, she answers. What a pleasant surprise. It's been a while.

It's strange the way something like the tenor of a person's voice can hit you in the soft spots of your body, spots you didn't know you had.

It has, I say.

She waits for more, so I just say, My father.

Is he ok? She asks.

I say nothing.

She says, Oh, Juan. I'm sorry. I am. Do you need to talk or someone to sit with? I can come over?

I nod but don't say anything. I keep nodding, and she stays on the line. She just listens and waits. I'm here, Juan.

I say, Thank you. I just needed to . . . I felt like you would want to know.

Of course, she says. Have you told Stella? Do you need me to? You know she loves . . . She needs to see you. You need to visit.

I know, I say. Betsy. I'm sorry that I behaved the way I did.

Tell her that.

I'm going to call her now.

Stella answers a bit breathless and asks if everything's ok. Her voice is really what I need. I ask how she's doing. I ask how Byron is just to keep her on the phone. I ask about her car, her classes, her job.

She is patient and responds to every question: she's good but busy, he's cute and funny, car's working but needs new tires, classes are tedious but necessary, job necessary but tedious.

I say, Welcome to the real world.

That's such a cliché, she says, but I know what you mean.

Stella, I'm thinking I can come down and see you. Meet Byron. Would you still want me to after. Well. I'm sorry.

Of course, dad. I think you'll like Byron.

I say, I need to tell you something. Your abuelo died a couple days ago. Your abuela called and told me this morning.

She says, Shit, Dad. Are you ok? How's Abuela?

I don't know. I'll know more when I go down there. But you should call her yourself.

Stella never knew my father. To her, he was a ghost.

Dad, I'm sorry about Abuelo. I know how horrible he was to you and all—

He wasn't that bad, I interrupt, not really knowing why.

She says, Whatever. But I sure am glad you're nothing like him. I love you, Dad.

She hangs up. I'm not sure how I feel. I work the rest of the afternoon, tying up loose ends, sending emails to people explaining I'll be unavailable for the next week.

Most clients are fine, but one is worried about their new website. They want to talk about it over the phone. A woman calls, and her voice is the opposite of my daughter or my ex-wife's. It's higher and flat like the sound of a computer malfunction. She wants assurances that if something goes wrong I'll be available.

Of course, I say, reassuring her with an ease that disturbs me, that reminds me of my father's promises.

Jason knocks on my door at about five. He has Chinese food with him, and he convinces me to text a few people and invite them to Nicks tonight as a way to mitigate the impact of the karaoke crowd, though neither one of us has been there on a Saturday.

I text Janet the acupuncturist. And tell her to bring her boyfriend. I text Betsy and say feel free to bring Stan. There is no one else to text.

Jason asks me about Jared. I say we haven't talked.

He refuses to drop the subject. You were really serious with him, right? Don't downplay, Juan.

I say with a slight smile, We were long-time lovers.

He says, Then it's even more important you let him know about your dad. You said that about Rosa and my accident. When shit like this happens, you need your people. These are the moments when you are reminded to put your shit down and step up. Give him that chance.

Jason made everything a do or die situation. I loved and hated this quality.

Call him, he says.

I hesitate.

Do it, he says.

I decide to text Jared, even though he hates that. I tell him that I'm going to San Jose for a week, that my father passed away, that I'm having a wake/support party at the bar, that I'd like to see him.

He immediately responds: I'll be there.

At Nicks I'm pounding sparkly water as fast as Bob can refill my glass. Janet is there with her boyfriend, Billy, a dapper-looking fortyish fellow with a deep voice and a meaty smile. Susan fidgets and mumbles under her breath because she wants karaoke to begin; Frankie, the oldest among us, posts up in the corner, dressed to the nines as usual; Betsy and Stan sip fancy cocktails in tall glasses; Jared swivels in the chair by the bar, back and forth, looking wonderful. It's Jason's first time back since his injury, so the regulars are excited to see him. He's joking about having pain medication to give away for anyone who needs it. Bob is wearing a suit and tie.

He says, It's poetry night tonight. I even brought a sonnet. I call it "Ode to Feelings."

I have a rush of anxiety and wonder if we should all leave right now.

I say, Really, that sounds horrible.

Bob snorts and says, You're lucky I'm not sensitive.

Shit, I meant that the poetry night sounds horrible. Not your poem.

I'm fucking with you, Juan. And trust me, the poem is meant to be horrible.

I call Jared off to the side. I feel like I should say something. Explain that I've missed him. That I'm glad, so glad, he's here. That I'm sorry.

He steps up to me, and as I start to speak he puts his fingers to my mouth. He says, Shush. Not now.

I try to respond.

Nope. Don't do it. I know you have so much to tell me. I know you've missed me. I know you regret everything. I know you realize you're chicken shit. But not now. Take me to lunch soon and beg me to take you back.

He slips his arms around my waist and hugs me, and I let him hold me. In a moment we return to the little group assembled at the back of the bar. Jason is saying why he loves any kind of creativity in public places. He says, You have to respect people's effort. I love when people at least try.

What don't you love? You're always so damn positive, I say.

He says, That's easy. I don't love hypocrites, pain, politicians, sellouts.

Jared says, Bananas.

Susan says, Professional sports.

Frankie says, The price of gasoline.

Bob says, Bad tippers and bad attitudes. He points at me but then smiles.

I feel like it's my turn, so I say, Fathers.

I am trying to make a joke, but it clearly bombs. There is this awkward moment of silence.

Finally Jason says, Trust me, Percocet can help with that.

Janet says, There's no acupressure point for fathers, but there is for cleansing and grief.

With that, Bob steps away to grab a PBR for someone, and we all begin talking again. Sometime later Betsy walks up to me and says, Juan, Stan and I need to leave, but we want to give you our condolences, and maybe I can make a toast with all your friends.

Before I can speak, Bob says, Yes. Hold on a minute. He sets out a row of shot glasses, grabs the bottle of Cazadores, and proceeds to pour shots for everyone.

This is on me, Bob says.

We pass them out, and everyone looks at me.

Betsy says, I met you when we were teenagers. I think I'm the only one here who's met your father. He was good-looking, very smooth, and such a jerk. Juan, you're like him in some ways, but one thing you are not is a jerk. I remember one of the very first things your father told me. He said that you were a good kid but he didn't know what kind of man you would be. He worried you might be a lost cause. Juan, he was so very wrong.

Frankie says, Hear, hear!

Jason says, Now that's a good story. To lost causes.

Everyone yells, To lost causes.

We raise our glasses high and hold them in the air for just a second. Long enough for me to see the sparkly way the lights refract through the glass and the liquor.

14

Love Regardless

The service is a quiet event at a Chávez's Funeral Home in Salinas. The body was cremated. I don't ask my mother how she feels, nor do I ask my father's surviving younger brother, Tio Sonny, a gregarious bear of a man with a smooth face and swath of wild black hair. He leans in and delicately embraces my mother, then steps to me. He shakes my hand before pulling me into a hug.

He says, He was a hard man. Stubborn and mean, pardon my honesty. But you were his best thing. I know he probably never told that to you. But he believed it. And I do too. You got family here, son. Don't hesitate to reach out.

It's the most meaningful thing I heard all during the service. All I can do is nod.

That evening, my mother asks, What are you going to do with the ashes?

Me?

He's your father.

He's your husband.

You can leave them here if you want, but you should really take them.

I don't say another word about it. We eat in silence.

In the morning, I pack up to continue driving down the 101 heading toward Los Angeles. Toward my daughter.

Just before I leave, I walk to the ashes. They are in a plain ceramic urn. I open it and grab a plastic bag.

My mother walks me to the door.

Tell Stella I love her, and mijo, I love you too. You are a good man.

We hug, my father in a plastic bag between us.

I drive out of Salinas. Into the morning. I push my car faster and faster. About twenty miles later, as I reach the outskirts of town, I roll down the window and grab the bag. With one hand on the wheel, I use my teeth to open the Ziploc. I don't taste anything, but I feel grit on my lips. Then I extend my arm into the wind. When the bag flaps loose against the doorframe, I let it go.

The drive on I5 to LA sucks. Hours of monotony. I look out the window at the burnt brown fields of the Central Valley. The cows huddle in packs under the sporadic oak trees. There is the constant hum of traffic, the intermittent distraction of exits and billboards and fast food restaurants.

I'm pushing eighty mph with this anxiety that sits in my belly, recalling what Betsy had told me when she returned from visiting Stella.

She'd stopped by my apartment, the same apartment we used to all share, super tiny, but all of us together. Betsy reported they were surprisingly grounded. They reminded her of us as a young couple, in love, arrogantly confident, and hopeful.

Sitting at our old kitchen table, she said, It's stunning how quickly things change, right? This is not what I expected from Stella. She leaned in and kissed my forehead. She said, Things worked out pretty damn well, in my opinion. We did good, Juan.

Betsy's face was tanned and wrinkled, hair graying but still full and long. It shocked me how she had aged, and yet how she still possessed the presence of that twenty-year-old woman I raised a child with.

When I pull up in front of Stella's apartment, I see my mother's old car. It's been washed. It has that green tree air-freshener hanging from the rearview mirror. It looks like a classic, like it's worth some money. Clearly someone's been taking care of it.

I knock on the apartment door. Stella opens it. I haven't seen her in six months.

Her hair is straight and thick and brown and pulled back into that familiar bun. Her skin looks a bit paler. Her face looks tired but content. There is this moment when you look at your child and can see them simultaneously as a baby and an adult. I recall that smile Stella had when she was so young and wild, and it's right there on her face. It's in the squint of her eyes. It's disturbing and beautiful and heartbreaking at the same time.

We lean toward each other in this tentative way. Then we hug, and I kiss the side of her head. Suddenly I'm hugging her harder, even picking her up off the ground, and saying, I love you so much!

It's then I feel her belly pressing into mine. I put her down immediately and look down at it.

I'm speechless. I want to touch the mound, but don't. I want to kneel before it and look closely, but don't.

She says, I know, right? I still can't believe it myself.

I take her hands in mine and try to give her a look that says everything, but she just stares back at me with growing uncomfortableness.

I am truly sorry for not being supportive. Not being there for you.

Dad, just because we were upset at each other doesn't mean it's the end of the world.

Do you forgive me?

I'm certain we can find a way for you to redeem yourself, she says and smiles. You want coffee?

I say, Sure.

I watch the way she makes it. She moves easily around the kitchen. She sets out a French press, three cups, and nothing else.

She says, Byron's in the shower.

You still drink it black? I ask.

She says, Black is so much easier. You were right about that.

I say, What was that?

You were right.

I'm sorry, but can you say that again?

She says, Haha. But then she laughs, and I never want her to stop.

I look around the apartment and see the way she has decorated it. There's nothing on the walls. The floors are clean. There's a complete lack of clutter. It's nothing like the chaos of her room when she lived with me, and I feel slightly hurt, offended.

I say, You're learning to clean up?

Not really, she says. You should see my room.

I say, I don't need to. I remember the mounds of clothes.

There're only a few mounds. I've changed. You know people change, right?

I say, I hope people change. But even as I speak these words, I realize that in my body it feels like the opposite is true. It feels like despite everything, nothing and nobody changes.

Byron enters and clearly hasn't been in the shower. I realize he's been hiding out, giving us some time. He looks part Asian, his black hair pulled back in a bun, and he's dressed in a casual but cool way, jeans a bit tight, funky old shirt, a cardigan sweater. He wears his jeans rolled and cuffed so you can see colorful socks and a pair of Keds.

Hello, Father, he says with a big smile, which gives him cute chubby cheeks.

I stand and extend my hand, which he totally ignores. Instead he steps toward me and gives me a big hug. I feel him rest his head on my shoulder for a second.

It's an honor to meet you, he says.

So, tell me about your family? I ask.

Dad, Stella barks.

Oh, Stella, relax. I'm just curious. I don't know anything. Just humor me and tell me the basics?

Of course, Byron says, and we all sit down. He clears his throat like he has prepared a response.

I grew up in Modesto. Been in LA a couple years. Met Stella at work. I had to train her. She asked a lot of questions, but I never had to correct anything she did after the training.

He reaches over to her forearm and touches it.

That's impressive, he continues. She's a natural at the register and customers love her.

Are you planning on going to school? I ask.

Not any time soon, he says and picks up his cup like he's done talking.

So that's the plan? Work at Wild Oats?

Yep, coolest name ever, he says, seeming content with his performance.

I can't help but smile at his genuineness.

Stella, I ask. And you?

Work and school and then transfer.

It's obvious neither wants to mention the baby, and I'm wise enough to avoid the subject, even if I can't stop my eyes from drifting to Stella's belly. Well, I say. Seems like you two have a great plan.

They give me a tour of the small apartment, a tour of the neighborhood, and we spend the evening talking about Stella's classes and my father's funeral and Betsy and Stan. It's easier than I expected, so good to see Stella. I surprise myself by sleeping well in the unfamiliar bed.

The next day at the obstetrician's office, we all sit in the waiting room, and Stella's nervous. She keeps checking her phone, then putting it down, then picking it up.

I say, Do you want some water or something?

She says, No, I'm fine.

I look at Byron, who's reading on his phone, casually sipping water out of a Dixie cup from the water dispenser.

She says, I just hate these things.

Doctor's offices? I ask.

No. More like just the meaning of a visit to the doctor. The power they have. It's like they are these oracles or something and what they say can totally change your life, you know?

She sounds a bit panicky, lost in some existential moment. Again I look at Byron, who's still sipping and reading. His demeanor bothers me as much as it attracts me. He seems so relaxed. I want to pull out my phone and get on my Scrabble game, but I don't dare.

I say, You should perhaps give up coffee at this stage. You seem a bit anxious. Byron, what do you think?

He looks up at me and then at Stella, and he smiles, and she smiles, and her shoulders drop a bit, loosen. Like that was what she needed, a smile from Byron, who then goes back to reading his phone.

There is another couple sitting across from us. They look to be in their thirties. He flips through a sports magazine, she through a New Yorker. They look comfortable. She has a huge belly. I see her and Stella make eye contact and smile at each other. I try to imagine my daughter with that big belly, with a child moving inside of her.

I whisper, It's ok to be scared, you know. I don't think you'll get that big.

She looks at me like I've said something offensive.

I say, I mean, it's totally ok if you do. Nothing changed in her expression. Perhaps I should just be silent. Perhaps Byron is onto something. Now I pull out my phone.

The woman across from us gets called in, and the man leans over and kisses her and says, Call me if you need me. Love you.

He watches her go back to the exam rooms and then sees me watching him. He nods at me like the woman did to my daughter. I smirk back. Then Stella gets called. I stand to go with her, but she says, Wait here.

She and Byron walk toward the exam room holding hands.

I sit back down. I pick up magazines. I put them down. I realize there's no music. I wonder why the silence. It seems like a little music would help soothe people waiting.

The man across from me says, I don't like to go in, either. I get all freaked out. He asks, When is she due?

I say, I'm her father.

I figured, the guy says. Must be even more intense in some ways. Being a grandfather and all. Remembering her as a child, and now here she is, all grown up herself.

I think of my daughter as a child and as a grownup and how similar it all is. How frightening. I want to shut it out, shut him out, but I resist the urge. It is intense, I say. I don't really know what to feel.

He says, Everything changes now.

What do you mean? I ask.

He says, For me it was hearing that heartbeat. When you realize there's a baby in there. A real baby. You can't deny a heartbeat. You can't be ignorant after that.

He laughs to himself. His clothes show he must work outdoors. He has a puffy, untrimmed beard that Jared would hate but Jason would probably love. He wears sunglasses on the brim of his baseball cap.

He asks, Can you remember hearing your daughter's heartbeat for the first time? Bro, I was blown away. I'll never forget that. Never.

No one has ever asked me that question, but I do remember. I remember Betsy and me in an office just like this one. I remember the doctor asking, *Do you want to listen to the baby's heart?* Betsy just smiled as she listened. I was the one who got teary eyed, who looked up to the doctor for confirmation that everything would be fine, that everything would be ok.

I stand up and walk to the door. I open it and ask the nurse, Where's my daughter?

I say, I want to see her.

The nurse says, Wait here. I'll go check in on the patient.

I feel my stomach tighten and I want to say something mean. Instead I say, She's not a patient. She's my daughter.

The nurse comes back in a minute and says, Your daughter said you can go on back. I knock on the door the nurse points to and ask, Stella, can I come in?

The doctor opens the door and says, Mr. Gutiérrez. Nice to meet you.

Hi, I say. Yes. Nice.

Your daughter is a picture of health. She's really prepared. You must be proud.

I don't say anything, but I look at the doctor and try to convey a *thank you*. I look at Stella, lying on the table with her belly out in the open. Her pregnant belly. I see her bellybutton is pierced and I feel a rush of anger. Another thing she kept from me. Byron sits next to her. They're still holding hands.

I breathe deeply and ask, Can I feel the baby?

Her forehead creases, but she nods.

I rub my hands together to warm them. I put my palms on her belly. I close my eyes. I feel nothing but a hard knot right under the skin. But then Stella puts her hands on my hands. They are warm. They feel strong and rough. I don't want to move.

The doctor interrupts us and says, Do you want to know the sex of the child?

No, Stella says with a firm shake of her head. Her eyes meet Byron's, and I can see they understand each other in that moment,

that they are speaking even while silent. I have a surge of something like envy.

Byron says, It doesn't matter. We'll love the baby either way.

He shifts forward and places his hands on top of hers, which are
on top of mine, which are on the belly. I see he has a tattoo of an S
on his ring finger. I wonder if it's for Stella. I think about what he
just said. I think about how we love things regardless of how little
we know about them, or how much. It's the bravest, craziest thing
anyone can do. Love despite what you know. Love because of what
you know. Love someone else. Love regardless.

15

With White People Come Problems

That's what Frankie says. He says it like it there's no arguing about it, his lanky body lounging in his same chair at the corner of the bar, his tall gin and tonic held in his hand like a scepter, the glass slowly beading with condensation.

He's talking about the young black man shot by the police on 63rd and King last Saturday night. Supposedly the officers stopped a bunch of men slowly biking through the streets. The news article used words like *detain*, *aggression*, phrases like *lack of cooperation* and *crime surge*. The result: one shot twenty-two-year-old male.

I'm at the bar both earlier than usual and on a Sunday, because I knew about the protest, and I knew both Frankie and Susan would be here having a drink once it was over. The music is low. The lights are on. The carpet's discoloration is obvious. Usually only the older, regular clientele are here this early, but today the bar is full because the person shot was born and raised in this neighborhood.

It also disturbs me how easily Frankie makes this statement. Like he's not even shocked. Like he saw it coming. Like it will come again. With me he's always been so amiable, nonchalant even. To-night, with all these people he's known for so long, he is much more animated. I've never seen him so alive. He moves his mouth like an old man without teeth.

He says, Every damn neighborhood I ever lived in that white people with kids arrive soon gets more police, and then soon gets someone shot or killed by the police.

Susan, dressed in black, says, I wish it wasn't true, but Frankie, you're true. You're too true.

I listen to her talk, this woman who dresses like every day is Sunday, sings an amazing array of '70s songs, drinks red wine, and takes care of twin grandkids. I look at Frankie, who never bends to drink but always lifts the glass to his lips. It's elegant. I remember the stories he's shared: traveling in the Alps and going to Carnival in Rio. Watching them, I feel invested in something I can't name.

I look around this bar I've called my bar for so long. Bob who wants to be a poet. Jason who models nude for art students. There are a few other familiar faces.

Despite my sense of belonging, I realize I have ignored opportunities to make closer connections. I remain content to know snippets. Bits and pieces. Never the whole story about someone.

Jason suddenly stands and hugs Frankie. I'm taken aback by this display of intimacy. Jason doesn't know Frankie any more than I do, but Frankie lets Jason comfort him. I see Frankie give in to it. I see Frankie hug him back.

You a good man, Jason, Susan says.

Jason says, It must be devastating. How well do you know the young man?

Frankie says, Since he was baby. He was no angel, but no one deserves to get shot on the street. Don't care if he stole a bike or not.

There has been a rash of break-ins in the neighborhood, and someone recently got held up on the corner right by Nicks. Because of this I met the new owner of Mr. Delbert's house, who approached me a couple of weeks ago as I passed the place.

Mr. Delbert's chain-link fence had been replaced with a new wooden one. The correct word would be *repurposed*. The beautiful weathered redwood made me both envious and angry. It was seven feet tall, and flowerpots, chartreuse and glossy, with geraniums overflowing and trailing down, topped each support beam.

I felt ashamed of the dry patch of grass and the garden boxes, weedy and abandoned now, in front of my apartment complex.

As I walked by, the gate slid open, and a man extended his hand.

I've seen you around, he said. Neighbors should know each other. I'm Patrick.

I'm Juan, I said.

Lived here long?

A while.

So you know a lot of people here. We were wondering about this group of kids that runs through the streets around dusk. Do you know them?

I shook my head.

There had been a time when I knew all the kids, a time my daughter and I would walk to school and say hello to mothers and uncles and grandmas and other kids walking to school. I remember walking Stella to Malcolm X. Remember the first year she told me she wanted to walk to school alone, and I said, *Of course,* wanting to trust her autonomy, but then stood there in front of our apartment and watched her walk the four long blocks, and every time she turned back, I waved like a fool so that she asked me to not watch her again. I agreed, but for the next month I hid in the bushes. I still see many of those kids, now grown. But the young ones, they're new to me.

We're having a meeting, Patrick said, of people in the neighborhood who are concerned about crime and safety. Would you want to come?

I don't think so, I said.

If you change your mind, we have a Facebook page, the New Life in South Berkeley group. Look for it.

Later I looked at the Facebook page. The way it described my neighborhood was like a tourist attraction. They used phrases like *family friendly* and *up and coming commercial corridor.* Words like *vibrant* and *safe.* They mentioned the word *safe* eight times. They referenced Temescal to the south and downtown Berkeley to the north. Like we were smack dab in the heart of everything.

Frankie and Susan are talking about the neighborhood using different words, telling different stories, like how Fairview Street has trees along only one side of it because the city council decided in the '90s to chop the other side down in an effort to thwart drug dealing and kids hanging out. To make it easier to police.

Jason and I just listen when Jared walks in.

Officially my boyfriend again.

After my father's funeral and my trip to LA, I waited a couple of painfully long weeks before reaching out. Seeing Byron and Stella, their ridiculous love, their obliviousness to all the real-world crap heading their way, was, in fact, inspiring. But it didn't make me delusional. I understand that the issues between Jared and me haven't gone away. I know people don't really change. They accept. They tragically and knowingly accept.

When I finally called, Jared answered, Hello Juan. His voice expectant. Eager, even.

This made me more nervous. The stupid ball was in my court again. I had practiced some potential conversation starters: *It meant a lot to me that you came to Nicks.* And, *It was a pleasure to see you, and perhaps we can have a coffee and chat.* And even, *It's been a minute. Should we hang out again?* It all sounded like a bad pop song.

So I told myself to just be honest. I told myself to trust my gut, which said I was hungry for something satisfying. But I didn't want to make false promises, either. Or proclamations of being better or different.

I just wanted to see him again.

I wanted to figure out if we could work.

I wanted a second chance.

Hello, Jared, I said. I'm calling to say I'm sorry.

Jared made a sound like he was thinking. I imagined the way he cocked his head to the side when he pondered something. I tried to picture him in his nook, comfortable and happy. Then in his tighty non-whiteys, stretched across his bed.

Look, if you're calling in sincerity, then I appreciate the apology. If you're looking for a booty call, I'll have to sadly decline.

I immediately felt guilty for the image in my head of him in underwear, but gathered myself and said, Sounds like you've really considered our options.

I don't like to waste time, especially on things that are—to be honest, totally honest with you, Juan—a bit scary and hard.

I was silent for a second. Then I said, I'm sorry for a lot, and I would like to talk with you about that and some other things.

Things? Jared pressed.

Us. You and I. Can I take you on a walk? Somewhere we can talk?

I would like that, he said. And as fast as it started, the conversation ended.

I picked him up on Sunday morning in my Mercedes. I had in my pocket a Sharpie to use if everything went right. I wore a matching gray sweat suit for our hike, casual and comfortable.

He sauntered out from his apartment carrying a backpack, dressed like we were getting brunch and a glass of wine.

I was thinking Albany Bulb, I said, but now I feel a bit under-dressed.

He jumped in and said, You're perfect and look very comfy. Now, onward.

You're in a good mood.

I'm hopeful.

The Bulb was a wasteland of cement and steel left behind from building I-80 and had become an overgrown, unincorporated anomaly: part park, part homeless encampment, part artist canvas. I used to take Stella there to see the wild structures people created out of ocean debris and other found materials, some of them huge—castles and forty-foot statues and mosaics on tree trunks. It was also a place kids went to hone their graffiti art on discarded cement slabs. Itd been peacefully cohabited until recently, when the City of Albany began *cleaning it up.* Clearly a euphemism.

Jared and I strolled to the edge of the bulb. The water was still and calm, and the air felt equally motionless. All through the walk, we dodged people with their dogs off leash. The area was one of the few remaining where that was still possible. We'd discussed Stella, whose due date was rapidly approaching, my father's funeral and my mother and Jason's broken arm and Nicks. When I stopped to turn around I said, I think I want a dog.

Jared said, That's random. Why?

I thought of Mr. Dog and how I called him a monster but Mr. Delbert called him a baby. I thought about how perhaps he was a little bit of both.

I said, What I really want is a second chance.

And that's an interesting segue. I'm not going to ask what all transpired in that brain of yours that lead you to that connection: dog and boyfriend. But let me ask again, why?

What could I say that didn't sound trite? I thought of my mom realizing she was wrong. I thought of Jason's ideas about happiness. I thought of Janet's finger in my mouth. I thought of kissing in the red light of barroom hallways and coming home to an empty house. I thought of Christmas lights and stupid religious statues.

I said, I wish there was a clear reason. There isn't. Only that I would like to try again. I think for me some things have changed.

Not all. I can't promise to be something I'm not. In fact, I won't promise to be anything except honest and kind.

Jared's face was beautiful but closed. He tilted his head and said, I need you to let me know when things are getting hard for you. When you're feeling afraid. I think with you, Juan, there is so much fear. But I won't be shut out anymore. You understand what I'm saying?

I think so. I can try, I said. I won't panic again, and I'll try not to push you away. I'll do my best to talk to you about what's going on with me.

He said, Deal. That's all I've ever really wanted. But someday you should think about what you are afraid of, what makes you so scared.

I squared off. I said, Why are you so brave?

I'm not. I didn't mean to sound like I've got my shit together. I don't.

Then what are you afraid of?

Loving you.

I exhaled like I'd been punched.

Jared said, But it wouldn't be any easier with anyone else. I know that. I've been dating lots of people for a long time, never wanting more than a good time. Or wait—if I'm being honest, I should say I was afraid of wanting the good times to become something deeper. I'm not anymore.

I don't know if I'm ready for some big serious thing.

I know that too. And so it may not work. I'm willing to try, but the one thing I'm not willing to do is try on my own. Just don't shut me out. Be brave and talk to me. Tell me what's going on. Give me a chance to participate in what happens.

He reached out and grabbed my sweat pants, but instead of pulling me close, he stretched them out wide. We both laughed.

I feel ridiculous in these, I admitted.

But they allow for some nice access, he said, and I felt his cold hands on my warm ass cheeks.

We sat on a slab of concrete painted pink, looking out at the bay with the Golden Gate Bridge in the distance and the Bay Bridge to the left of us. It was perfect. He grabbed a bottle of French rosé from his backpack and said, I know you don't drink wine that much, but drink this with me.

I said, Uncork that bad boy.

He said, Don't need to. It's a twist off.

We gulped straight from the bottle, and I caught up on his life, the bullshit job drama. We talked about the bad dates we both went on, the things we missed about each other.

He admitted he missed the way I made coffee.

See, I yelled.

I admitted I missed the way he held me when we slept.

There's no drinking here, a voice said. We turned to see two cops on bikes.

I said, No problem. We're leaving.

You don't have to leave. But you can't drink alcohol.

As they pedaled away, Jared whispered, I hate how nervous I get when they pop out of nowhere. I was afraid to move my arms. We're two people of color with no cameras around breaking the law.

Point taken.

Well, maybe one and a half. You got that white privilege skin.

Well then, I said and unscrewed the cap, drank, and passed the bottle to Jared.

So dangerous, he said and sipped.

I remembered the Sharpie tucked into my sock. I retrieved it and on the slab of cement that we sat on, I wrote: *On this day Juan promises to try.*

Jared said, That's the most romantic declaration of love I have ever witnessed. Jared wrote underneath my scrawl: *On this day Jared promises to try as well.*

Now I look at Jared in the god-awful blue-hued lighting of Nicks, dressed in business slacks and a button-up shirt with shiny leather shoes, and I wonder why I ever let go of him.

He says, I parked in front of your apartment and just walked here, not that I'm expecting you to take me back to your place later.

He gives my neck a kiss, and I feel it in my freshly trimmed balls. An ache. A hunger.

Jared turns to Frankie and Susan and says, Can I buy you two lovely people a drink?

Susan says, There's lots of things to say no to, but a drink isn't one of them.

Jared looks at Bob, and Bob nods. Bob is all grace. He knows tonight it's important to keep people happy.

Jared turns to me and says, I just yelled at a bunch of kids who busted up somebody's flowerpots.

What? I say. Are you serious?

Yeah, he says. I used my *you don't want to mess with me* voice. Gave them my crazy eyes. It actually works.

He smiles, proud he can scare a bunch a teenagers.

You're so intimidating. I smirk.

He says, Don't you forget it.

Jason is asking questions. He's sitting with Frankie, Susan, this huge guy with a Cal hat on, a few other people that I've seen before but don't know by name. Jason wants to know what this area was like in the '70s with all the political stuff happening, and in the '90s, when the war on drugs was at its height. Bob leans up against the counter, listening. It's still early and karaoke doesn't begin for another few hours.

Frankie says, This bar was a social club back in the day. Every Sunday used to have a table lined up with crock-pots.

Susan says, All along that wall. She points to where the karaoke machine is set up, with small sheets of crumpled white paper littering the carpet below it.

There was a grill in the back too, Frankie says, crossing his arms.

You could get a lot more than food back in the day, the huge guy with the Cal hat says.

He laughs, and Susan and Frankie join him. Clearly they know each other. Clearly they have history.

I know what you're talking about, Frankie nearly shouts, leaning back like the memory is grand and huge.

Jason asks, What about the Black Panthers. Did they come around here?

He asks all in awe and excited.

The Cal hat guy says, This wasn't a place for them. They were too young. They all met at the coffee shop by the old Merritt College. Close, but not here. Only people who hung out here were a bunch of hustlers.

They all start talking loudly and over each other.

Jason turns to us and says, It feels like shit to be part of gentrifying a neighborhood, causing its history to be erased.

Jared says, Don't look at me. No matter how queer I am, I'm still black and male. I'll never make a neighborhood safe.

True, Jason says.

See, Jared says to me. That's why I can scare people.

I say, That's not it. It's your hustler-like demeanor.

Jared kicks my foot.

Jason says, But I meant me and punks and activists. We move into cheap neighborhoods. We make them safe, even though we think of ourselves as allies. It's really fucked up when you think about it.

I'm not sure what to say. I think of moving here so long ago. People told us not to rent here because it wasn't *family friendly*.

Jason says, There has got to be a way for me to move into a neighborhood and not ruin it.

No one answers.

Jared and I decide it's time to say our goodbyes. When I go up to Frankie, I take a page from Jason's book and hug him. I do the same to Susan. Maybe what makes a neighborhood is a willingness to hug your neighbor.

Jared and I head out. As we walk, I reach for his hand. We are silent until we turn the corner, and Jared says, Oh, shit. Look. That must be the person who lives there, the place with the flowerpots I told you about.

I know immediately who it is: Patrick, the man who lives in Mr. Delbert's old house. He has a flashlight in his hand.

When he sees it's me, he waves, the beam piercing the night sky. We approach, and he trains the beam on the mess.

I look at the potting soil on the ground. I can see the chartreuse sheen of the broken pots mixed in with rich brown of the dirt.

Jared says, I saw who did it.

You did? Patrick turns to him.

Yes, I interrupt. These two drunk white dudes.

Are you serious? Patrick says.

Jared looks at me with a *what the hell you doing* expression. I ignore him.

Patrick shakes his head, his body crumpling like those slips of paper surrounding the karaoke machine.

He says, I don't understand people sometimes. It's just so disappointing. So disappointing, he repeats.

I say, Guess you should probably call the cops now, I say like an accusation or like I'm proving something.

No, no, Patrick says. That will only cause more problems. It's just a plant.

I can feel Jared's attention on me, and I stare at Patrick as Jared reaches out and pats his shoulder.

He says, I'm sorry.

Patrick nods and says, Thank you. He bends down to start cleaning up. Jared joins him. I watch them sift through the dirt and gather the plants. Jared and Patrick each pick out a few and cradle them.

Patrick says, I can save these. They aren't so bad.

Jared says, I think you can probably save them all.

They both hustle through the gate and across the yard like time is of the essence. I bend down and start picking out the pieces of pottery. I make a small pile next to the gate.

Patrick returns and says, I love that color.

I say, Me too. Perhaps you can do something with the pieces.

When we leave, Jared whispers, Sometimes people surprise you. He starts to run toward my complex down the street, pulling me with him as he bounds across the dead front lawn and over the garden boxes. He hurries up the steps and stands at the top stair, looking a little like Frankie, confident, regal. Like he knows something important, something true. Like tonight all the kids will be safe on their bikes, and no one will get hurt. I smile up at him when I reach the stairs and take them two at a time, jumping into his embrace.

16

The Sexiest Letter in the Alphabet

It's almost three in the morning, and I'm wide awake. This is unusual. I'm what you would call an early bird: in bed by ten, thirty minutes of reading, thirty minutes to masturbate, five to clean up, asleep by eleven, give or take a few minutes. Like clockwork. Of course, when Stella was with me, the masturbation wouldn't happen. But I was ok with that. The last thing I wanted was to be caught by my daughter. Now that she's gone, the only thing that prevents me from masturbating is Jared. When he spends the night, it's hard to masturbate and impossible to sleep. Sex with him is wonderful, but masturbating is also important and part of my routine, part of what helps me get to sleep.

Jared snores next to me. His sleeping face looks delicate and exposed. I place my hands on his head, but he doesn't stir. He just keeps on slumbering. I want to be irritated, to blame him for my lack of sleep, but I'm trying to be more honest with myself, so I breathe deeply and focus on the fact that my birthday's coming up. For many this would be a happy thought, but I hate birthday stress.

In the morning, Jared brings me coffee.

He says, Drink up, grandpa. You look terrible.

I say, You would too if I kept you up all night.

Maybe it's just because you're getting old, grandpa, he says.

Ever since Stella had Joaquin, he calls me grandpa whenever he can. It's officially my nickname. Even Jason uses it. Even Bob and Frankie and Susan and Betsy. Jared knows I love Joaquin fiercely, but hate to be called grandpa, so he uses the term with relish.

I'm still getting used to the idea that I have a grandson. It happened quickly. A week before Stella's due date, at 5 in the morning, she sent a text that read *Dad hurry the baby's coming.* I jumped up, tossing clothes into the suitcase while Jared made me coffee, despite the fact he had to work in a few hours and could easily have remained in bed. He drove me to the airport calmly, humming some soft tune and asking pleasantly distracting questions: did I need him to reserve a rental car? Reserve a hotel room? He was so sweet that as we pulled up, I asked him what was going on.

He ignored my attempt to deflect and said, Are you ready for what's coming?

I think I'm fine, I said. I just hope she's ready.

You are such an adorable abuelo. Now go get the little whippersnapper.

I kissed him on the lips, coffee breath and stubble and nervousness all mixed up in my affection.

All through the plane and taxi rides to the UCLA Medical Center, I kept grinning. I told anyone who would listen that I was about to be a grandpa: the person sitting next to me working on Excel spreadsheets, who stopped to high-five me; the flight attendant, who proceeded to make an announcement over the intercom that resulted in cheers; the taxi driver who asked if he should hurry, and I said *as fast as you can, my man*; and finally the person at the information booth, who had just arrived for their shift but dropped everything to give me my visitor badge and walk me to the elevator.

I felt special. Loved. Even by strangers.

I stormed into the delivery room, and Betsy shushed me because

Stella and Byron slept. It had been a long night. The contractions were intermittent but intense. Betsy's face was wet with tears. I leaned down and kissed her cheeks. I turned to Stella and put my hand on her head. Her skin was sweaty and flushed.

I whispered, You have everything you need right here, and I kissed her forehead.

To Betsy I said, Should I wait outside, or do you think she'd mind if I watched?

You're certainly a wonderful father, but get the hell out.

The doula and doctor entered just as Stella woke with a low growling noise and Byron jumped up and held her arms.

I love you, Stella. I'm right outside if you want me back in here. I looked at Betsy, who shook her head and began to breathe in time with Stella.

Thank you, Dad, Stella yelled with the contraction.

I sat in the bland waiting room watching some news channel on mute. About thirty minutes later the doula walked in and asked, Would you like to meet your grandson?

I smiled, and for the first time since I could remember, I cried.

Now, two months after the birth, a few days before my fortieth birthday, Jared standing beside me as I'm lying in bed, I feel so strangely happy and anxious.

Jared asks, Hey, you all right? Anything you want to talk about?

I take a sip of his coffee, and it's weaker than I like, but I say, Thank you.

He sits next to me, looking puzzled, like a dog does when it lifts its ears and tilts its head. I think of Mr. Dog. I wonder if he's still alive. When I pass the old Delbert house now, instead of howling at Mr. Dog like I used to, I say hello to Patrick or his wife when one of them is out in the front with their baby. She toddles along the sidewalk after me.

I say to Jared, Don't give me that sad dog face.

He says, Let's start again. Good morning. It's officially the beginning of your birthday week. What would you like to do?

I say, I wish sometimes you understood me enough to just figure it out. I sip the coffee, making loud slurping sounds that I know irk Jared.

He says, It helps if you tell me what's going on. I know you have a thing about birthdays.

This time I give him the sad dog face. Not surprisingly, he acts like he doesn't know what I mean and kisses me on the cheek.

Try not to get all weird over the next couple days, ok? he says. He turns and begins his morning routine.

The next day, while peeing at the Actual Café, where I'm meeting Janet for a birthday coffee, I play my pee game, in which I alternate holding my cock with the left had then the right then the left and so on until I'm finished urinating. Nine times out of ten, the hand holding the cock at the end is the right. It's strangely scientific. As I wash my hands, I notice someone has written in the grout between tiles little messages all playing off the word *grout*. One that stands out to me is *groutuitous*. I return to my table and decide to list the lovers I've had over the last few years: 1. Jose 2. Julia 3. Elijah 4. Jared. Feeling slightly disappointed that there are only four, I discover the preponderance of the letter *J*.

The next evening, we're at a work party for Jared's Green and Brown Institute, a celebration for an award given to them by the state of California. It's at a bar, so I'm posted up next to the bartender, an old gentleman in a suit that reminds me of Frankie. He's generously pouring me cheap California wine. It's big and buttery, a phrase he says over and over, like a mantra. I realize I like the phrase as well: *big and buttery*.

I spot Jared across the room, standing in a group of three men in gray business suits and colored dress shirts. They all look big and buttery. He looks in my direction, and I smile at him. I realize it's easier to share my desire for him from twenty feet away than face to face.

When he saunters up to me, I say, You're sexy like a California chardonnay.

He looks at me like I've had one too many California chardonnays. I want to explain he's big and buttery, but realize that might not come off right, so I refrain.

He says, I think you should move in with me.

I stare blankly at him, but he seems fine to just wait me out.

I say, What's your philosophy on splitting communal purchases if we break up?

His eyes full of pleasure, he says, Fifty/fifty. You can have all the souvenirs from our travels, but the records are mine.

I say, I don't share underwear.

He says, Why would I wear your underwear?

I say, You ask that now.

We clink wine glasses.

Over the next hour I listen to Patti and Damian and Jared affectionately tease each other.

Back at my place, Jared sits next to me, leaning on his elbow and resting his head on his hand as he looks at me, not blinking. I feel like prey.

He says, Put your phone down.

It's about ten thirty. I am beginning to fidget. He puts his hand on my cock. I open my online Scrabble game. He kisses my chest. My letters are *akejfco*. I try to play *jackoff* using the *f* from the word *often*. It's denied. I know it's two words, but I had hope.

He asks, Juan, does this bother you?

I say, Your hand on my cock? No, absolutely not.

He says, No, me asking if you want to move in.

I say nothing. He grabs my phone out of my hand.

He says, Listen, Juan. Gramps. You need to check yourself right now. I will not start playing these games. You hear me?

I lean into his belly and say, Sorry.

What? He asks.

Sorry, I repeat.

He says, My hearing must be playing tricks on me.

I put my phone away and slide down to him and we don't say another word.

Three days later, it's my birthday and I'm at his apartment. All the rooms are immaculate, '70s chic, with an attention to coordination and detail matched only by IKEA showrooms. Wood candle holders, brown and blue ceramics, and his precious nook. I try to imagine how it would change if I were to call this place home.

He puts on an Elliott Smith album and says, I love it when you put on a record and remember how good it is.

I say, You always put on this one. You know he's got like twelve other albums.

Eight, he corrects. And only five while he was alive.

Jared sways to the music. He puts his thumb out like a microphone and mouths: *They took your life apart and called your failures art.*

Why do you love this hipster white boy so much? I ask.

Elliott was way before hipsters. He might in fact be the O.H. The original hipster.

He says this with such sincerity I feel slightly aroused.

Jared puts his thumb mic down and says, Juan, listen to the way he sings. Listen to how honest he is, like he has nothing to hide, like his heart is wide, wide open.

Then Jared tells me to kiss him.

I fight the urge to protest, walk to him and raise his arms. Smell the scent of his armpits. I say, I am sorry about being so high maintenance. Tell me where to kiss you exactly.

He tilts his head and says, I have a few places in mind. But it's *your* birthday.

It is, I say.

He says, I want to take you to dinner. Nothing fancy, because I know you don't like fancy. We can go to Saturn. After that we can do whatever you want. We can go to Nicks. We can come home. Whatever.

He says this like it's a gift.

I ask, If we move in together, would we go by Jared and Juan? Or Juan and Jared?

I can see he thinks it's a trick question, but he says, It's alphabetical always.

I feel happy and strange about it. I tease, I'm just trying to get a sense of things. I'm trying to see if we match up.

How's this? he says and he pulls me into him. Hip bone to hip bone, my slightly larger belly squished to his, my lips inches from his. Both our faces shaved clean.

He looks at me expectantly. Then his phone rings, and we both release each other.

He says, I need to take this, then walks into the other room.

Later that evening we get on our bikes to head to dinner, but first we agree to stop at Nicks for a birthday beverage. I love to ride after dark: the illuminated windows, the feel of the nighttime air, the way the neighborhood can be so quiet. We pedal along King side by side, taking up the road. It's arrogant, and I feel like the wide, wide world is all for us.

I'm a little disappointed because Jason's not at the bar, but Frankie and Susan and Bob are clustered at the far corner staring at a line of shot glasses on the bar top. The TV's off. The karaoke monitor's black. There's low jazzy music playing. They all smile when I come in.

Bob says, Perfect timing. Here's a new drink I'm working on. We're upping our cocktail game.

You're joking, I say.

Lay your eyes on the super fancy French 510.

171

How's that fancy? It sounds like a bad marketing scheme.

It's really just a French 75, but we're calling it the French 510.

Bob, I understand the name. I hope you didn't come up with it. And here you call yourself a poet.

Just try it, he says.

We all pick up our little shots of French 510 and throw them back, and the drink is, in fact, delicious.

What makes it 510?

Local lemons and gin from Alameda's Hangar 1.

Susan excuses herself, saunters up to the microphone, and plugs it in. At this point, she could run the karaoke evening herself.

Testing, testing, she sings.

We all look at her.

Jared, would you care to join me?

He gets up, and I give him a *what the fuck are you doing* look.

They stand together and sing the worst rendition of feliz cumpleaños I have ever heard. Frankie and Bob hum along. The few customers in the bar all join in and cheer me at the end. When we leave, I hug each person. Even the strangers. I think to myself to avoid the French 510s in the future because they are dangerous and get me all emotional.

On our ride to downtown, Jared asks me if I'll ever be comfortable thinking of us as a couple. He asks not in an antagonistic way, but in a curious way.

I think of explaining to him that there are those key moments in life, events that explain the way you are, the root causes of the quirks and fears you bear throughout your existence. For example, there's the time my mother, after slicing the tip of her finger off, cried quietly but continued to make dinner for my father, who was hungry and drunk and watching sitcoms.

Instead of telling him what I'm thinking, I say, simply, My mother and my father.

He reaches across the distance between our bikes, gives my shoulder a quick squeeze.

He suddenly howls, weaving his bike in the street, sitting up on his bike and letting go of the handlebars, and the sound is so loud and appealing that I begin to howl right along with him. I realize I can still sense his fingers on my shoulder, the places they touched.

Jared stops about a block away from the restaurant.

Why we stopping here? I ask.

No reason, he says and checks his phone.

We lock our bikes, and Jared acts giddy. He's smiling and seems so smugly pleased with himself that I say, What's a matter with you?

What's a matter with you, he mimics, puffing up his chest. Then he hugs me and runs ahead up the block. I take my time getting there, but he just waits, holding open the door of the restaurant.

As I step up to him, he says, Juan, happy birthday.

I walk through the door and see my daughter. I see my grandson, Joaquin, in her arms. I see Byron. I see Jason and a tall woman with short hair standing next to him. I figure this must be his girlfriend, Rosa.

They all yell, Happy birthday!

I feel my face getting hot. I want to say something to Jared, but he's hidden himself amid the group, and he's laughing.

Jason steps up and as he pulls me toward his companion, he says, Sorry I wasn't at the bar, but I figured you'd understand my excuse. I was picking up Rosa. Rosa, this is Juan. He's my best friend.

Rosa says, It's such a pleasure to meet you and your beautiful family. Your grandson is adorable.

I don't know how to answer, so I just say, Thank you.

I sit down, and we all just start talking. I hold Joaquin. I see Stella and Byron arguing over what to order. I watch Jared and Jason and Rosa congratulate themselves on pulling this off.

How long have you been here, Stella? I ask.

We drove up today. Mom rented us a fancy car because she didn't want us driving little Joaquin in mine. You know mom. We go back on Monday.

The baby is big and fat and has hair thick as a wig. There's enough of it to brush. Straight jet-black hair like his father's. But he also has this bald ring beginning around the back of his head from sleeping. Like a baby monk.

I watch my friends. They talk animatedly. I sense something in my body, but don't know what to call it.

I look at Jared and ask, What do you want to eat?

He points to the specials on the menu. I want the Space Cowboy, he says.

I say, Honey, don't we all.

True, he says. But then he asks, What do you want, Juan?

I can't really decide, so I smile and say, I wish I could have everything.

He looks at me like I've said something big, something important, and for once I don't shy away. I lean over and kiss him, a loud smack on the lips.

But for now, I continue, I'll take the crispy tofu salad.

He laughs, and I feel him touch my knee under the table.

I savor the weight of his hand as I look around the restaurant again with its bright pink walls and silver glittery pillars. It feels like something has happened, but no one seems to notice. In this moment, they laugh and talk and pass the baby around. Right in this moment, they all seem to feel so perfectly happy. And, I realize, so do I.

ACKNOWLEDGMENTS

I believe, as Ada Limón beautifully writes in her acceptance speech for the National Book Critics Circle Award for Poetry, that I too have never written anything alone:

I want to acknowledge my partner, Heidi Avelina, for her fearless trust, guidance, patience, and astute ability to offer criticism and encouragement.

I want to acknowledge my personal big familia: all the storytellers, the artists, the wild ones, the ones still here and the ones who have passed on.

I want to acknowledge my writing group—Ariel Gore, Michelle Gonzales, and Karin Spirn—writers committed to craft and community.

I want to acknowledge Nicola Mason and all the people at Acre Books for their work in helping bring this book to life. Shout out to my Press-mate Nancy Au for the willingness to imagine book tours and road trips. And thanks to Rob Moss Wilson for such beautiful art.

I want to acknowledge that my home and much of the setting for my writing is on the ancestral, traditional, and contemporary land of the Muwekma Ohlone people.

And finally, I confess, I love letters. Write me what you think, and I promise to write back....

Tomas Moniz
PO Box 3555
Berkeley, CA
94703